"It was a present. From a friend."

"A friend...." Hugo's eyebrows rose. "A *friend* and not your husband?"

"I don't *have* a husband," Dee gritted furiously.

"No husband!"

Something hot and dangerous flared in his eyes and Dee started to panic, but it was too late. The damage had already been done, the tinder lit.

"No husband," Hugo repeated thickly. "What did he do, Dee? Refuse to play the game your way...just like I did...?"

Dee gave a gasp and then made a small shocked sound as the pressure of Hugo's mouth on her own prevented her from saying *anything* else.

It had been so long since she had been kissed like this. So long since she had been kissed at all. Hungrily her mouth opened under Hugo's, and equally hungrily her hands reached for him.

Dear Reader,

Revenge is a very strong emotion. The need to seek it and the act of avenging a wrongdoing is very empowering. The four women in this, my latest, miniseries all have to learn to handle this most powerful of emotions, each in her own special way.

I am aware of the dangers of people becoming blinded to everything but one single, obsessive goal. As I wrote these four books, I discovered that my heroines, Kelly, Anna, Beth and Dee, all share my instincts. Like me, they desperately want to see justice done, but—also like me—they come to recognize that there is an even stronger drive: love can conquer all.

The four women share a bond of friendship, and it is very much in my mind when I write that you, the reader, and I, the writer, share a very special and personal bond, too. I invite you to share in the lives, hopes and loves of Kelly, Anna, Beth and Dee. Through love they will discover true happiness.

Love, laughter and friendship—life holds no greater joys, and I wish you all of them and more.

Penny Jordan

SWEET ~~REVENGE~~ *Seduction*

They wanted to get even. Instead they
got married!

PENNY JORDAN

The Marriage Resolution

SWEET ~~REVENGE~~ *Seduction*

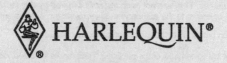

HARLEQUIN®

TORONTO • NEW YORK • LONDON
AMSTERDAM • PARIS • SYDNEY • HAMBURG
STOCKHOLM • ATHENS • TOKYO • MILAN • MADRID
PRAGUE • WARSAW • BUDAPEST • AUCKLAND

ISBN 0-373-12079-6

THE MARRIAGE RESOLUTION

First North American Publication 2000.

Copyright © 1999 by Penny Jordan.

Visit us at www.romance.net

Printed in U.S.A.

CHAPTER ONE

DEE LAWSON paused in mid-step to admire the pink and yellow stripes of the flowers in their massed corporation bed in Rye-on-Averton's town square.

She had just been to have coffee with her friend Kelly. Beth, Kelly's friend and business partner in the pretty crystal and china gift shop the two girls ran in the town—a property which they rented from Dee herself—had also been there, along with Anna, Beth's godmother. Anna's pregnancy was very well advanced, and she had laughed a little breathlessly as her baby kicked when his or her mother reached for another biscuit.

With Beth's wedding to Alex only weeks away Dee suspected that it wouldn't be very long before Beth too was blissfully anticipating the prospect of becoming a mother.

Strange to think that so little time ago motherhood had been the last thing on any of their minds.

Dee's eyes clouded a little. But, no, that wasn't quite true, was it. Motherhood, babies, children, a family were subjects which had always been close to her *own* heart, even if those feelings, that *yearning*, had in recent years become something of a closet desire for her, a sadness for what might have been had things been different.

She wasn't too old for motherhood, though, not at

thirty-one—Anna was older than her—and plenty of women in their thirties, conscious of the urgent tick of their biological clocks, were making the decision not to waste any more time but to commit themselves to motherhood even without a committed relationship with their baby's father.

Had she wanted to do so, Dee knew *she* could have quite easily and clinically arranged to conceive, even to the point of choosing the biological details of the male donor who would be the father of her child. But, strong though her maternal instincts were, Dee's own experience of losing her mother shortly after she was born meant that, despite the caring love she had received from her father, for her own child she wanted the extra-special sense of security and belonging that came from being a child surrounded by and brought up with the love of both its parents, for it and for each other. And that was something that was just not possible…not for her…not any more… Once, a long time ago, she had believed…dreamed…

But that had been before Julian Cox had wormed his way into her life, corrupting her happiness, destroying her security.

Julian Cox!

Her full lips twisted distastefully.

It was typical of the man that he had cunningly managed to escape the legal retribution which must surely have been his had he remained within the reach of European law. Where was he now? Dee wondered. She had tried through the considerable network of contacts at her disposal to find him. The last time there had been a firm sighting of him had been last year, in Singapore.

Julian Cox.

He had caused so much destruction, so much unhappiness in other people's lives, those people he had deceived and cheated via his fraudulent investment scams, people like Beth, and Kelly's husband Brough's sister Eve, vulnerable women whom he'd tried to convince that he loved purely so that he could benefit financially. Luckily both of them had ultimately seen through him and had found happiness elsewhere. For her things were not so simple. For her...

Dee stopped and glanced towards the elegant three-storey Georgian building from which the builders' scaffolding had just been removed, revealing it in all its refurbished splendour.

When she had originally bought it, the building had been in danger of having to be demolished, and it had taken every bit of Dee's considerable skill to persuade not just the planners but the architect and the builders she had hired that it could be saved, and not just saved but returned to its original splendour.

All the time and effort she had put into achieving its restoration had been well worthwhile, just for that wonderful moment when at a special ceremony the county's Lord Lieutenant had declared it officially 'open' and she had seen the name she had had recarved and gilded above the doorway illuminated by the strategically placed lighting she had had installed.

'Lawson House'.

And on the wall there was an elegant and discreet

scrolled plaque, explaining to those who read it that the money to purchase and renovate the house had been provided posthumously by her father in his memory. And it was in his memory that its upper storey was going to be employed as office accommodation for the special charities which Dee maintained and headed, whilst the lower ground floor was to be used as a specially equipped social area for people of all ages with special needs, a meeting place, a café, a reading room—all those things and more.

And above its handsome marble fireplace she had placed a specially commissioned portrait of her father, which the artist had created from Dee's own photographs.

'I wish I could have known him. He must have been the most wonderful man,' Kelly had once commented warmly when Dee had been talking to her about her father.

'He was,' Dee had confirmed.

Her father had had the kind of analytical brain that had enabled him to make a fortune out of trading stocks and shares. With that fortune he had philanthropically set about discreetly helping his fellow men. It was from him that Dee had inherited her own desire to help others, and it was in his name that she continued the uniquely personal local charity which he had established.

And it wasn't just his desire to help his fellow men that Dee had inherited from her father. She had also inherited his shrewd financial acumen. Her father's wealth had made her financially independent and secure for the rest of her life. Dee did not need to earn a living, and so, instead, she had turned her attention and her skills to the thing that had been closest to her father's heart after his love for her.

As the financial brain behind all the charities her father had established, as well as their chairperson, Dee had made sure that the charities' assets were secure and profitable—and, just as important, that their money was invested not just profitably but sensitively so far as not taking advantage of other people was concerned.

All in all, Dee knew that she had a lot to be grateful for. The friendship which had sprung up between her and the two younger women, Beth and Kelly, who rented the shop premises from her, and Anna, too, had added a very welcome and heart-warming extra strand to her life. Dee was part of a large extended family that had its roots in the area's farming community and which went back for many generations; she had the pleasure of knowing that she had faithfully adhered to all the principles her father had taught her, and that her father himself was remembered and lauded by his fellow citizens.

A lot to be grateful for, yes, but she still couldn't help thinking about when... But, no, she wasn't going to dwell on that—not today—not any day, she informed herself firmly. Just because seeing Anna's pregnant state and Beth and Kelly's happiness had made her so sharply conscious of the void which existed in her own life that did not mean...

Above her head the sky was a vivid spring blue decorated with fluffy white clouds whipped along by the breeze. The Easter eggs which had filled shop windows in recent weeks had been removed to make way for flowers and posters advertising the town's special May Day celebration, which had its roots in the ancient May Day Fair which had originally been held in the town in medieval times.

There would be a procession of floats, sponsored in the main these days by corporate bodies, a funfair in the town square, a bonfire and fireworks, and, since she was on the committee planning and co-ordinating the whole affair, Dee knew that she was going to be busy.

Amusingly, she had been shown an old document recently, listing the rules which applied to anyone bringing sheep, cattle or other livestock into the town on May Day. The modern-day equivalent was making rules for the extra volume of traffic the Fair caused.

Babies were still on Dee's mind when she eventually got home. A second cousin on her mother's side had recently had twins, and Dee made a mental note to buy them something special. She had heard on the family grapevine that she was going to be asked to be their godmother. It was a wonderful compliment, Dee knew, but, oh, how it made her heart ache. Just the mere act of holding those precious little bundles of love would make her whole body ache so!

In an effort to give her mind a different and more appropriate turn of direction, she decided that she ought to do some work. Strength of will and the ability to follow through on one's personal plans were, her father had always told her, very positive assets, and to be admired. Perhaps they were, but over the years Dee had become slightly cynically aware that so far as the male sex was concerned a strong-minded woman was often someone to be feared rather than admired, and resented rather than loved.

Dee switched on her computer, telling herself firmly that it was silly to pursue such unprofitable thoughts. But it was true, a rebellious part of her brain insisted on continuing, that men liked women who were illogical, women who were vulnerable, women who were feminine and needed them to help and protect them. *She* was not like that, at least not outwardly. For a start she was tall—elegantly so, her female friends often told her enviously. Her body was slim and supple, she enjoyed walking and swimming—and dancing—and she was always the first one her younger nieces and nephews wanted to join in their energetic games whenever there was a family get-together.

She wore her thick honey-coloured straight hair long, primarily because she found it easier to manage that way, often coiling it up in the nape of her neck in a style which complemented her classically elegant bone structure. Whilst she had been at university she had been approached in the street by the owner of an up-market model agency who had told her that she had all the potential to become a model, but Dee had simply laughed at her, totally unaware of the dramatic impact of her timeless elegance.

Over the years, if anything that impact had heightened, rather than lessened, and although Dee herself was unaware of it she was now a woman whom others paused to glance at discreetly a second time in the street. The reason so many men appeared to be intimidated by her was not, as she herself imagined, her strength of will, but in actual fact the way she looked. That look combined with the classically stylish clothes she tended to favour meant that in most men's eyes Dee was a woman they considered to be out of their league.

Dee frowned as she studied the screen in front of her. One of the new small charities she had taken under her wing was not attracting the kind of public support it needed. She would have to see if there was some way they could give it a higher profile. Somewhere for teenagers to meet, listen to their music and dance might not have the appeal of helping to provide for the more obviously needy, but it was still a cause which, in Dee's opinion, was very deserving.

Perhaps she should speak to Peter Macauley about it. Her father's old friend and her own retired university tutor shared her father's philanthropic beliefs and ideals. A bachelor, and wealthy, having inherited family money, he had already asked Dee to be one of the executors of his will because he knew that she would see that his wishes and bequests were carried out just as he would want them to be. He was on the main committee appointed by her father to control the funds he had bequested to finance his charities.

Thinking of Peter Macauley caused Dee to pause in what she was doing. He was not recovering from the operation he had had some months ago as quickly as he should have been, and the last time Dee had driven to Lexminster to see him she had been upset to see how frail he was looking.

He had lived in the university town all his adult

life, and Dee knew how strenuously he would resist any attempt on her part to cajole him into moving to Rye-on-Averton, where she could keep a closer eye on him, never mind how he would react to any suggestion that he should move *in* with her. But the four-storey house he occupied in the shelter of the town's ancient university was far too large for him to manage, especially with its steep flights of stairs. He had friends in the town, but, like him, they were in the main elderly. Lexminster wasn't very far away, a couple of hours' drive, that was all...

It had been Dee's first choice of university, since it had offered the courses she'd wanted to take, and, more importantly, had meant that she wouldn't have to move too far away from her father. In those days the new motorway which now linked the university town to Rye had not been built, and the drive had taken closer on four hours than two, which had meant that she had had to live in student digs rather than commute from home.

Those days... How long ago those words made it seem, and yet, in actual fact, it had only been a mere ten years. Ten years...a different life, a lifetime away in terms of the girl she had been and the woman she was now. Ten years. It was also ten years since her father's unexpected death.

Her father's death. Dee knew how surprised those who considered themselves to be her closest friends would be if they knew just how profoundly and deeply she still felt the pain of losing her father. The pain—and the guilt?

Abruptly she switched off her computer and got up.

Seeing Anna had done more than reawaken her own secret longing for a child. It had brought into focus things she would far rather not dwell on. What was the point? What was the point in dwelling on past heartaches, past heart*breaks*? There wasn't one. No, she would be far better employed doing something productive. Absently—betrayingly—she touched the bare flesh of her ring finger, slightly thinner at its base than the others. Other things—such as what?

Such as driving over to Lexminster and visiting Peter, she told herself firmly. It *was* a couple of weeks since she had last seen him, and she tried to get over at least once a fortnight, making her visits seem spur-of-the-moment and accidental, or prompted by the need for his advice on some aspect of her charity work so as to ensure that his sense of pride wasn't hurt and that he didn't guess how anxious she had become about his failing health.

Her sleek car, all discreet elegance, just as discreetly elegant as she was herself, ate up the motorway miles to Lexminster, the journey so familiar to her that Dee was free to allow her thoughts to drift a little.

How excited she had been the first time she had driven into the town as a new student, excited, nervous, and unhappy too, at leaving her father.

She could still vividly remember that day, the warm, mellow late-September sunshine turning the town's ancient stone buildings a honey-gold. She had parked her little second-hand car—an eighteenth-birthday present from her father—with such care and pride. Her father might have been an extremely wealthy man, but he had taught her that love and loyalty were more important than money, that the truly worthwhile things in life could never be bought.

She had spent her first few weeks at university living in hall and then moved into a small terraced property, which she had co-bought with her father and shared with two other female students. She could still remember how firm her father had been as he'd gone over the figures she had prepared to show him the benefits of him helping her to buy the cottage. He had known all the time, of course, the benefits of doing so, but he had made her sell the idea to him, and she had had to work too, to provide her share of the small mortgage payments. Those had been good years: the best years of her life—and the worst. To have gone from the heights she had known to the depths she had plummeted to so shockingly had had the kind of effect on her that no doubt today would have been classed as highly traumatic. And she had suffered not one but two equally devastating blows, each of which...

The town was busy; it was filled with tourists as well as students. All that now remained of the fortified castle around which the town had been built were certain sections of carefully preserved walls and one solitary tower, an intensely cold and damp place that had made Dee shiver not just with cold but with the weight of its history on the only occasion on which she had visited it.

Economics had been her subject at university, and one which she had originally chosen to equip her to work with her father. But there had always co-existed within her, alongside her acutely financially perceptive brain, a strong streak of idealism—also inherited from her parents—and even before she had finished her first university term she had known that once she had obtained her degree her first choice of career would be one which involved her in using her talents to help those in need. A year's work in the field, physically assisting on an aid programme in one of the Third World countries, and then progressing to an administrative post where her skills could be best employed, had been Dee's career plan. Now, the closest she got to helping with Third World aid programmes was via the donations she made to their charities.

Her father's untimely death had made it impossible for her to carry on with her own plans—for more than one reason. Early on, in the days when she had dutifully taken over the control of his business affairs, there had been a spate of television programmes focusing on the work of some of the large Third World aid organisations. She had watched them with a mixture of anguish and envy, searching the lean, tanned faces hungrily, starving for the sight of a certain familiar face. She had never seen him, which was perhaps just as well. If she had...

Dee bit her bottom lip. What on earth was she doing? Her thoughts already knew that that was a strictly cordoned-off and prohibited area of her past, an area they were simply not allowed to stray into. What was the point? Faced with a choice, a decision, she had made the only one she could make. She could still remember the nightmare journey she had made back to Rye-on-Averton after the policeman had broken the news to her of her father's death—'a tragic accident,' he had called it, awkwardly. He had only been young himself, perhaps a couple of years older than her, his eyes avoiding hers as she'd opened the door to his knock and he'd asked if she was Andrea Lawson.

'Yes,' she had answered, puzzled at first, assuming that he was calling about some minor misdemeanour such as a parking fine.

It had only been when he'd mentioned her father's name that she had started to feel that cold flooding of icy dread rising numbingly through her body.

He had driven her back to Rye. The family doctor had already identified her father's body, so she had been spared that horrendous task, but of course there had been questions, talk, gossip, and despite the mainly solicitous concern of everyone who'd spoken with her Dee had been angrily conscious of her own shocking secret fear.

Abruptly Dee's thoughts skidded to a halt. She could feel the anger and tension building up inside her body. Carefully she took a deep breath and started to release it, and then just as carefully slid her car into a convenient parking spot.

Now that the initial agonising sharpness of losing her father had eased Dee wanted to do something beyond renovating Lawson House to commemorate his name and what he had done for his town. As yet she was not quite sure what format this commemoration would take, but what she did know was that it would be something that would highlight her father's generosity and add an even deeper lustre to his already golden reputation. He had been such a proud man, proud in the very best sense of the word, and it had hurt him unbearably, immeasurably, when...

She was, Dee discovered, starting to grind her teeth. Automatically she took another deep breath and then got out of her car.

In the wake of the arrival of the town's new motorway bypass there had also arrived new modern industry. Locally, the town was getting a reputation as the county's equivalent to America's silicone valley. The terrace of sturdy early Victorian four-storey houses where Peter lived had become a highly covetable and expensive residential area for the young, thrusting executive types who had moved into the area via working in the new electronics industries, and in a row of shiny and immaculately painted front doors Peter's immediately stuck out as the only shabby and slightly peeling one.

Dee raised the knocker and rapped loudly twice. Peter was slightly deaf, and she knew that it would take him several minutes to reach the door, but to her surprise she had barely released the knocker when the door was pulled open. Automatically she stepped inside and began, 'Goodness, Peter, that was quick. I didn't expect—'

'Peter's upstairs—in bed—he collapsed earlier.'

Even without its harshly disapproving tone the familiarity of the male voice, so very, very little changed despite the ten-year gap since she had last heard it, would have been more than enough to stop her dead in her tracks.

'Hugo...what...what are *you* doing *here*?'

As she heard the trembling stammer in her own voice Dee cursed herself mentally. Damn! Damn! Did she *have* to act like an awestruck seventeen-year-old? Did she have to betray…?

She stopped speaking as Hugo started to shake his head warningly at her. He pushed open the old-fashioned front-parlour door and indicated that she was to go in.

Obediently Dee did so. She was still in shock, still grappling to come to terms with his unexpected presence. It was years since she had last seen him.

When they had first met he had been a graduate whilst she had still been a first year student. He had been working towards his Ph.D., a tall, quixotically romantic figure with whom all her fellow female students had seemed to be more than half in love. Even in a crowd as diverse and individual as his peers had been, Hugo had immediately stood out—literally so. At six foot three he had easily been one of the tallest and, it had to be said, one of the best-looking men on the campus, so strikingly and malely attractive that he would have automatically merited a second and a third look from any woman, even without his signature mane of shoulder-length thick dark hair.

Add to the attributes of his height and male physique—tautly muscled from playing several sports—the additional allure of shockingly sensual aquamarine eyes and a mouth with the kind of bottom lip that just automatically made a woman know how good it would be to be kissed by him, and it was no wonder that Hugo had been the openly discussed subject of nearly every female undergraduate's not-so-secret fantasies.

Dee had quite literally run into him as he was rushing to one of Peter's meetings one day.

Dee, who had heard about Hugo from the female grapevine, and who had glimpsed him to heart-stopping effect in and around the campus, had been astounded to discover that Hugo was a leading activist in Peter's small army of idealists and helpers.

'What do you mean, what am I doing here?' Hugo was challenging her now curtly. 'Peter and I go back a long way and—'

'Yes, yes, I know that,' Dee acknowledged. 'I just thought…'

She was in shock; she knew that. Her body felt icy cold, and yet at the same time as sticky and uncomfortable as though she was drenched in perspiration. Her heart was hammering frantically to a disjointed and dangerously discordant rhythm, and she suspected that she was actually in danger of hyperventilating as she tried to force some air into her tense lungs.

'You just thought what?' Hugo demanded tauntingly. 'That I was still carrying a torch for you? That I just couldn't go on living without you any longer…that my feelings for you, my love for you, was so strong that I just had to come looking for you…?'

Dee blenched beneath the witheringly sardonic tone of his voice. Was it really unbearably cold in this room or was it her…? She could feel herself starting to tremble. Only inwardly and invisibly at first, and then with increasing intensity until…

'How are your husband and your daughter?' Hugo asked her with obvious indifference. 'She must be…how old now…nine…?'

Dee stared at him. Her *husband*…her *daughter*… What husband…what daughter…?

Someone was knocking on Peter's front door.

'That will be the doctor,' Hugo announced before she could gather her confused thoughts and correct his misapprehensions.

'The doctor…?'

'Yes, Peter is very poorly. Excuse me, I'll go and let her in.'

Her! Peter's normal doctor wasn't a woman!

As she stood to one side a very attractive, cold-eyed brunette walked through the door towards Hugo, saying, 'Ah, Mr Montpelier. I'm Dr Jane Harper; we spoke on the phone.'

'We certainly did,' Hugo agreed, with far more warmth in his voice than there had been when he'd spoken to her, Dee noticed, digesting the unwanted recognition that knowledge brought as uncomfortably as though it had been a particularly unwelcome piece of food.

'Please, come this way,' Hugo was inviting the doctor, and she was smiling at him as though…

Angrily Dee swallowed down her own unpalatable thoughts.

CHAPTER TWO

PETER was very poorly. She had known he wasn't well, of course, and had been getting increasingly concerned about him, but to hear Hugo describing him as 'very poorly' had come as an unpleasant shock to her. Anxiously Dee followed Hugo down the narrow hallway. She had seen the female appreciation in the other woman's eyes as Hugo had let her in, even if it had been quickly masked by her professionalism as she'd asked quickly after her patient.

She herself was quite obviously an unwanted third, Dee recognised as Hugo outlined Peter's symptoms to the doctor and she listened intently to him, positioning herself so that Dee was blocked out of Hugo's line of vision. Not that she minded that. She was still trying to come to terms with the shock of his totally unexpected presence.

The last time she had seen him he had been a rangy young man dressed in tee shirt and jeans, his wild mane of hair curling youthfully round his face. Initially his reputation as something of a rebel had caused Dee's father to be a little bit disapproving of him, but even her father could not have found fault with the appearance he presented now, Dee acknowledged as his absorption with the doctor gave her the opportunity to study him surreptitiously. The tee shirt and jeans had been exchanged for a smartly tailored business suit, and the dark hair was no longer shoulder-length but clipped neatly to his head, but the bone structure was still the same, and so were the aquamarine eyes and that dangerously sexy mouth. Dee's heart gave a dangerous little flutter—and that was something else which did not appear to have changed either!

Anxious to distract herself, as well as concerned for Peter, she started to walk towards the stairs.

'Where are you going?' Hugo demanded, breaking off his quiet conversation with the doctor.

'I thought I'd go up and see Peter...' Dee began, but immediately both the doctor and Hugo began to shake their heads in denial.

Feeling thoroughly chastised, Dee tried to conceal her chagrin.

'I'd better go up and see him,' the doctor was saying to Hugo.

'Yes. I'll come with you,' he agreed.

Both of them were totally ignoring Dee. To suffer such ignominy was a totally unfamiliar experience for her, and not one she was enjoying, but there was no way she intended to leave—not until she had discovered how Peter was.

It was ten minutes before the doctor and Hugo came back downstairs, and Dee's anxiety for Peter overcame her outraged pride enough for her to ask quickly as they walked into the room, 'How is he? What's wrong with him? Will...?'

'He's got a weak heart and he's been overdoing things,' the doctor told her matter-of-factly. 'Trying to move some books, apparently. He really shouldn't be living on his own, not at his age. He ought to be living in some kind of sheltered accommodation since he doesn't appear to have any family, and in view of his recent operation.'

'Oh, no, that would be the last thing he would want...' Dee began to protest. but the doctor was already turning away from her.

'He was fortunate that you were here when he collapsed and that you knew what to do,' she said warmly to Hugo. 'If he'd continued to try to lift those books...' She stopped, and Dee told herself sternly that she was being unfair in thinking that what Hugo had done was quite simply what any person with any sense would have done, and scarcely seemed to warrant his elevation to the rank of a super-hero as the doctor seemed to suggest.

'I'll make some arrangements with the social services for some home help for him,' the doctor told Hugo, once again totally excluding Dee from the conversation.

'Oh,' she added, suddenly turning to glance dismissively at Dee. 'He wants to see you...'

'I told him you were here,' Hugo informed her briefly as Dee hurried towards the door.

Was she being unkind in suspecting that the doctor wanted to have Hugo to herself? And if she did what business was it of hers? Dee thought as she hurried upstairs.

Peter looked very small and frail lying there in bed, the sunshine pouring through the open windows highlighting the thin boniness of his hands.

'Peter!' Dee exclaimed warmly as she sat down

beside him and reached for one of his hands, holding it tightly.

'Dee, Hugo said you were here... Now, you're not to worry,' Peter told her before she could say anything. 'Hugo is just fussing. I just felt a little bit short of breath, that's all. There was no need for him to call the doctor...

'Dee...' Suddenly he looked very fretful and worried. 'You won't let them send me...anywhere...will you? I want to stay here. This is my home. I don't want...'

Dee could see how upset he was getting.

'Peter, it's all right. You're not going anywhere,' Dee tried to reassure him.

'The doctor was saying that I ought to be in a home,' Peter told her anxiously. 'I know. I heard her...she...'

He was starting to get even more upset, increasing Dee's concern for him.

'Peter, don't worry...' She started to comfort him, but as she did so the bedroom door opened and Hugo came hurrying in, glowering at her as he strode protectively to Peter's side.

'What have you been saying to him?' he demanded acerbically. 'You're upsetting him...'

She was upsetting him? Of all the nerve.

'Peter, it's all right,' she promised her father's old friend gently, deliberately ignoring Hugo—not an easy feat with a man the size Hugo was, and even less easy when one took into account his overpowering sexual charisma. 'The only home I would ever allow you to move into would be mine, and that's a promise…'

Out of the corner of her eye Dee could see the way Hugo's mouth was tightening.

What was he doing here anyway? She had had no idea that Peter still had any contact with him. He had certainly never mentioned Hugo to her.

'I don't want to go anywhere; I want to stay here,' Peter was complaining fretfully, plucking agitatedly at the bedcover as he did so. Dee's tender heart ached for him. He looked so vulnerable and afraid, and she knew, in her heart of hearts, that for his own sake he ought not to be left to live on his own. Somehow she would have to find a way to persuade him to come to live with her, but he would, she knew, miss his university friends, the old colleagues he still kept in touch with.

'And staying here's exactly what you shall do—at least so long as I have any say in the matter,' Hugo told him firmly.

Dee glowered at him. It was all very well for Hugo to make promises that were impossible to keep. And as for him having any say in the matter…!

But before she could say anything, to her astonishment she heard Peter demanding in a shaky voice, 'You are going to stay here, then, are you, Hugo? I know we talked about it, but…'

'I'm staying,' Hugo agreed, but although he said the words gently the look in his eyes as he looked across the bed at her made Dee feel more as though he was making a threat against *her* than a promise to Peter. What on earth was going on? What was Hugo doing here? There were so many questions she wanted—*needed*—to ask Peter, but it was obvious that he was simply not well enough to answer her—and that knowledge raised other concerns for Dee.

Peter shared with her the legal responsibility for administering the charities her father had established, and, whilst technically and practically speaking the work involved was done by Dee, via her offices in Rye-on-Averton, so far as legally rubber-stamping any decisions was concerned Peter was her co-signatory, and his authority was a legal requirement that had to be adhered to. He, of course, had the right to nominate another person to take over that responsibility for him, and Dee had always assumed that, when the time came, they would discuss who would take on that duty. Now it seemed it could well be a discussion she was going to have to have with him rather earlier than she had expected.

Peter was a gentleman of the old school, with the old-fashioned belief that women—'ladies'—needed a strong male presence in their lives to lean on, and Dee knew that he secretly deplored the fact that she had never married and had no husband to 'protect' her. She suspected too that he had never totally approved of the licence and authority her father had left to her so far as his financial interests went, and she often wondered a little ruefully what Peter would have thought had he known that her father had appointed him as a co-trustee for Peter's benefit and protection rather than for hers.

'His ideas, his ideals are more than praiseworthy,'

her father had once told her, adding with a sad shake
of his head, 'But...'

Dee had known what her father meant, and very
tactfully and caringly over the years she had ensured
that Peter's pride was never hurt by the realisation
that her father had considered him to be not quite as
financially astute as he himself believed he was.

In less than a week's time Dee was due to chair
the AGM of their main committee. There were certain
changes she wished to make in the focus and operation of her father's local charity, and she had been
subtly lobbying Peter and the other members of the
committee to this end.

Her main aim was to focus the benefit of the rev-
enue the charity earned, from public donation and the
endowments her father had made to it, not on its present recipients but instead on the growing number of
local young people Dee felt were desperately in need
of their help. Her fellow committee members, people
of her father's generation in the main, would, she
knew, take some convincing. Conservative, and in
many ways old-fashioned, they were not going to be
easy to convince that the young people they saw as
brash and even sometimes dangerous were desperately insecure and equally desperately in need of their
help and support. But Dee was determined to do it,
and as a first step towards this she needed to enlist
Peter's support and co-operation as her co-signatory.

She had already made overtures to him, suggesting
that it was time for them to consider changing things,
but it would be a slow process to thoroughly convince
him, as she well knew, and she had sensed that he

was already a little bit alarmed by her desire to make changes.

Peter had fallen asleep. Quietly Dee stood up and started to move towards the bedroom door, but Hugo got there first, not just holding it open for her but following her through and down the stairs.

'There's really no need for you to stay here with Peter,' Dee began firmly once they were both downstairs. 'I could—'

'You could what? Move him into your own home? What about your own family, Dee...your husband and child? Or is it children now? No, Peter will be much more comfortable where he is. After all, if you'd genuinely wanted him there you'd have taken steps to encourage him to live with you before now, instead of waiting until he's practically at death's door...'

Death's door! Dee's heart gave a frightened bound.

'I *did* try to persuade him,' she defended herself, ignoring Hugo's comment about her non-existent husband and family in the urgency of her desire to protect herself from his criticisms. 'You don't understand...

Peter's very proud. His friends, his whole life is here in Lexminster...'

'You heard what the doctor said,' Hugo continued inexorably. 'He's too old and frail to be living in a house like this. All those stairs alone, never mind—'

'It's his *home*,' Dee repeated, and reminded him quickly, 'And you heard what he said about wanting to stay here...'

'I heard a frightened old man worrying that he was going to be bundled out of the way to live amongst strangers,' Hugo agreed. 'At least that's one problem we don't have to deal with in Third World countries. Their people venerate and honour their old. We can certainly learn from them in that respect.'

Third World countries. It had always been Hugo's dream to work with and for the people in such countries, but a quick discreet look at his hands—lean, strong, but not particularly tanned, his nails immaculate—did not suggest that he had spent the last ten years digging wells and latrines, as they had both planned to do once they left university.

How idealistic they had both been then, and how furiously angry Hugo had been with her when she had told him that she had changed her mind, and that it was her duty to take over her father's responsibilities.

'You mean that money matters more to you than people?' he had demanded.

Fighting to hide her tears, Dee had shaken her head. 'No!'

'Then prove it...come with me...'

'I can't. Hugo, please try to understand.'

She had pleaded with him, but he had refused to listen to her.

'Look, if I'm going to stay here with Peter there are one or two things I need to do, including collecting my stuff from my hotel. Can you stay here?'

The sound of Hugo's curt voice brought Dee abruptly back to the present.

'Can you stay here with him until I get back?'

Tempted though she was to refuse—after all, why should she do anything to help Hugo Montpelier?—

'Hasn't he told you? He's the chief executive in charge of a very special United Nations aid programme. As I understand it, from what he's told me, their plan is to educate and help the people they're dealing with to become self-sufficient and to combat the ravages of the years of drought their land has suffered. He's very enthusiastic about a new crop they're still working on, which, if it's successful, will help to provide nearly forty per cent of the people's protein requirements.'

'That *is* ambitious,' Dee acknowledged.

'Ambitious and expensive,' Peter agreed. 'The crop is still very much in the early experimental stages. The whole scheme involves huge amounts of international funding and support, and one of Hugo's responsibilities is to lobby politicians for those funds. He was saying that he'd much prefer to be working in the field, but as I reminded him he always did have a first-class brain. At one time I even thought he might continue with his studies and make a career in academics himself, but he was always such a firebrand...'

A firebrand. Dee had thought of him more as a knight in shining armour, rescuing not distressed damsels but others less fortunate than himself and with far more important needs. Being romantic and idealistic herself, it had seemed to her that Hugo had met every one of her impossibly high ideals and criteria, morally...emotionally...and sexually... Oh, quite definitely sexually! Her virginal reluctance to commit herself physically to a man had been totally and completely swept away by the passion that Hugo

her concern for Peter was too strong to allow her to give in to the temptation.

'Yes, I can stay,' she agreed.

'I'll be as quick as I can,' Hugo told her, glancing frowningly at his watch. A plain, sturdy-looking one, Dee noticed, but she also noticed that it was a rather exclusive make as well. His clothes looked expensive too, even if very discreetly so. But then there had always seemed to be money in Hugo's background, much of it tied up in land, even if he had preferred to make his own way in his university days. His grandmother had come from a prosperous business family, and she had married into the lower levels of the aristocracy.

In Hugo's family, as in her own, there had been a tradition of helping others, but Hugo had dismissed his grandfather's 'good works' as patronage of the worst kind.

'People should be helped to be independent, not dependent, encouraged and educated to stand free and proud...'

He had spoken so stirringly of his beliefs...his plans.

Dee longed to reiterate that he had no need to concern himself with Peter, that *she* would take full responsibility for his welfare, but she sensed that he would enjoy dismissing her offer of help. She had seen the dislike and the contempt darkening his eyes as he'd looked at her, and she had seen too the way his mouth had curled as he had openly studied her as she crossed Peter's bedroom floor.

What had he seen in her to arouse that contempt?

Did he perhaps think the length of her honey-blonde hair was too youthful for a woman in her thirties? Did he find her caramel-coloured trousers with their matching long coat dull and plain, perhaps, compared with the clothes of the no doubt very youthful and very attractive women *he* probably spent his time with? Did it amuse him to see the way the soft cream cashmere of her sweater discreetly concealed the soft swell of her breasts when he had good reason to know just how full and firm they actually were?

What did it matter *what* Hugo thought? Dee derided herself as he turned away from her and strode towards the door. After all, he had made it plain enough just how little he cared about *her* thoughts or her feelings. She shivered a little, as though the room had suddenly gone very cold.

Ten minutes after Hugo had left Dee heard Peter coughing upstairs. Anxiously she hurried up to his room, but to her relief as she opened his bedroom door she saw that he was sitting up in bed, smiling reassuringly at her, his colour much warmer and healthier than it had been when she had seen him earlier.

'Where's Hugo?' he asked Dee as she returned his smile.

'He's gone to collect his things,' she answered him. It hurt a little to recognise how eager he was to have the other man's company—and, it seemed, in preference to her own.

'How are you feeling?' she asked him. 'Would you like a drink...or something to eat?'

'I'm feeling fine, and, yes, a cup of tea w very welcome, Dee.' He thanked her.

It didn't take her very long to make it, a carried the tray upstairs to Peter. In addition to she had made him some delicately cut little wiches, as well as buttering two of the home scones she had brought with her for him. She he had a weakness for them, and couldn't help ing at the enthusiasm he exhibited when he saw

'I didn't realise that you and Hugo had k touch,' she commented carefully when she was ing his tea. He had insisted that he didn't either or want to go back to sleep.

'Mmm... Well, to be honest, we hadn't...did But then I happened to run into him a few m ago quite by chance. He was here in Lexmins business and we were both guests at the same do. I wasn't sure it was him at first...but then h over and introduced himself.'

'Mmm...he has changed,' Dee agreed, ben head over the teapot as she poured her ow hoping that her voice wasn't giving her a would have recognised Hugo anywhere— some things that were just too personal changed. The aura that surrounded a pe which one knew instinctively once one h mitted within their most intimate person scent, as highly individual as their fir even the way they breathed. These w could not be changed.

'What's he actually doing these quired as carelessly as she could.

had aroused in her. Utterly, totally and completely. She hadn't so much as timidly crossed her virginal Rubicon as flung herself headlong and eagerly into its tumultuous erotic flood!

'You should talk with him, Dee,' Peter was continuing enthusiastically. 'He's got some very good ideas.'

'Mmm... I hardly think learning to grow our own protein is a particularly urgent consideration for the residents of Rye,' Dee couldn't resist pointing out a little dryly.

It irked her a little to be told she should crouch eagerly at Hugo's feet, as though he were some sort of master and she his pupil. In fact, it irked her rather more than just a little, she admitted. She might not have completed her degree course—her father's death had put an end to that—and she had certainly not been able to go on to obtain her doctorate, but what she had learned both from her father and through her own 'hands-on' experience had more than equipped her to deal proficiently and, she believed, even creatively with the complexities and demands of her own work. So far as she was concerned she certainly did not need Hugo's advice or instruction on how to manage her business.

'You've got a definite flair for finance,' her father had told her approvingly, and Dee knew without being immodest that he had been quite right.

She also knew she had a reputation locally for being not just astute but also extremely shrewd. Her father, on the other hand, had been almost too ready to trust in other people's honesty, to believe that they were as genuine and philanthropic as he himself had been, which was why…

'Dee, you aren't listening to me,' Peter was complaining tetchily.

'Oh, Peter, I'm sorry,' Dee apologised soothingly.

'I was just saying about Hugo, and about how you would be well-advised to seek his advice. I know your father was very proud of you, Dee, and that he meant it for the best when he left you in charge of his business affairs, but personally I've always felt that it's a very heavy burden for you to carry. If you'd married it might have been different. A woman needs a man to lean on,' Peter opined.

Dee forced herself not to protest. Peter meant well, she reminded herself. It was just that he was so out of step with modern times. It didn't help, of course, that he had never married, and so had never had a wife or daughter of his own.

'By the way, did you ever find out what had happened to that Julian Cox character?' Peter asked her.

Immediately Dee froze.

'Julian Cox? No…why do you ask?' Warily she waited for his response.

'No reason; it was just that Hugo and I were talking over old times and I remembered how badly your father was taken in by Cox. That was before we knew the truth about him, of course. Your father confessed to me—'

'My father barely knew Julian,' Dee denied fiercely. 'And he certainly had no need to confess anything to anyone!'

'Maybe not, but they were on a couple of charity

committees together. I remember your father being very impressed by some of Julian's ideas for raising money,' Peter insisted stubbornly. 'It was such a tragedy, your father dying when he did. To lose his life like that, and in such a senseless accident...'

Dee's mouth had gone dry. She always hated talking about her father's death. As Peter was saying, it had been a tragic, senseless way to die.

'Hugo said as much himself...'

Dee felt as though her heart might stop beating.

'You were discussing my father's death with Hugo?'

The sharp, shocked tone of her voice caused Peter to look uncertainly at her.

'Hugo brought it up. We were talking about your father's charity work.'

Dee tried to force herself to relax. Her heart was thudding heavily as anxiety-induced adrenalin was released into her bloodstream.

'I'm a little bit concerned about this bee you've got in your bonnet about these young people, Dee,' Peter was saying now, a little bit reprovingly. 'I'm not sure that your father would have approved of what you're trying to do. Being philanthropic is all very well, but these youngsters...' He paused and cocked his head. 'I applaud your concern for them, but, my dear, I really don't think I can agree that we should fund the kind of thing you've got in mind.'

Dee's heart started to sink. She had always known it would be difficult to convince Peter to support what she wanted to do, and the last thing she wanted to do now was to upset him by arguing with him. She had no idea how serious his condition might be, and she suspected that any attempt on her part to find out would be met with strong opposition from Dr Jane Harper. If it were Hugo, now, who wanted to know…! She was being unfair, Dee warned herself mentally—unfair and immature. But that didn't mean that she wasn't right!

'What exactly *is* Hugo doing in Lexminster?' she asked Peter, trying to give his thoughts a new direction.

'It's business,' Peter told her vaguely.

'Business?' Dee raised her eyebrows. 'I thought you said his work involved lobbying politicians for international support for his aid programme.'

'Yes. It does,' Peter agreed. 'But Lexminster University has access to certain foundation funds which have been donated over the years to be used as the university sees fit.'

'For charitable causes,' Dee agreed. She knew all about such foundations.

'Hugo hopes to get the university to agree to donate all or part of them to his aid programme.'

'But *I* thought they were supposed to be used to benefit university scholars' projects.'

'Hugo *was* a university scholar,' Peter reminded her simply. Yes, he had been, and Peter was on the committee that dealt with the disbursement of those funds, as Dee already knew. She started to frown. Was Hugo's desire to move in with Peter and take care of him as altruistic as it had initially seemed? The Hugo she had known would certainly never have stooped to such tactics. But then the Hugo she had

known would never have worn a Savile Row suit, nor
a subtly expensive and discreet cologne that smelled
of fresh mountain air just warmed by a hint of citrus.

Dee was becoming increasingly alarmed at the
thought of leaving Peter on his own with Hugo, but
she sensed that it wouldn't be wise to express her
doubts. From what Peter had already said to her it
was obvious that for him Hugo could do no wrong.

Dee was frowning over this unpalatable knowledge
when she heard someone knocking on the front door.

'That will be Hugo!' Peter exclaimed with evident
pleasure. 'You'd better go and let him in.'

Yes, and no doubt lie prone in the hallway so that
he could wipe his boots on her, Dee decided acidly
as she got up off the bed.

CHAPTER THREE

'How's Peter?' Hugo asked Dee tersely as she opened the door to him.

'He seems a lot better, although I'm sure that Dr Jane Harper would be delighted to give you a much more professional opinion if you wanted one,' Dee responded wryly, forcing herself not to wince as Hugo's glance swept her from head to foot with open dislike.

'It's odd how one's memory can play tricks on one. I had a distinct memory of you being an intelligent woman, Dee.'

'Well, I'm certainly intelligent enough to wonder what it is that makes *you* so anxious to help Peter.'

As Dee stressed the word 'you' she could see the anger flashing like lightning in Hugo's eyes. It gave her an odd, sharp stab of pain-tipped pleasure to know that she had drawn such a reaction from him, even whilst she had to force herself to blot out of her memory the knowledge that once there had been a time when that lightning look had been born of the urgency of his desire *for* her, instead of the urgency of his ire *against* her.

'I am anxious to help him, as you put it, because it concerns me that he should so obviously be on his own,' Hugo replied pointedly.

'He isn't on his own; he's got me,' Dee protested fiercely.

Immediately Hugo's eyebrows rose.

'Oh...? He told me that the last time he had seen you was over two weeks ago.'

Angrily Dee frowned.

'I try to see him as often as I can, but—'

'Other people have a prior claim on your time?' Hugo suggested. 'Be honest, Dee, *you* couldn't have moved in here to take care of him, could you?'

'He could have come to Rye with me,' Dee protested, without answering his question. 'And if you hadn't been here he would have.'

'He would? Yes, I'm sure he would. But would that have been what he really wanted? He wants to stay here, Dee. This is his home. His books, his things, his memories...his *life*...are all here.'

'Maybe, but you can't stay with him for ever, can you, Hugo? And what's going to happen to him once you've gone?'

'Since, for the foreseeable future, I'm going to be based in the UK, there's nothing to stop me from making my home here in Lexminster if I choose to do so. It's convenient for the airport and—'

'You're planning to live *permanently* in Lexminster...?'

Dee couldn't help her consternation from showing in her voice, and she knew that Hugo had recognised it from the look he gave her.

'What's wrong?' he taunted her. 'Don't you *like* the thought of me living here?'

'No, I don't,' Dee told him truthfully, too driven

by the way he was goading her and the shock of what he had just told her to be cautious or careful. 'I don't like it at all.'

'Oh, and why not, I wonder? Or can I guess? Could it have something to do with this…?'

And then, before she could guess what he intended to do, he had dropped the hold-all he was carrying and pinned her back against the wall, his hands hard and strong on her body as he held her arms, his body so close to her own that she could feel its fierce male heat engulfing her.

Once, being held like this by him would have thrilled and excited her, her awareness of the danger he was inciting only heightening her intense desire for him. The sex between them had been so passionately explosive that for years after he had gone she had still dreamed about it…and about him, waking up drenched in perspiration, longing for him, aching for him; and now, like a faint reflection of those feelings, she could feel her body starting to shudder and her nipples starting to harden beneath the practical protection of her jumper.

'Cashmere… Do you know how many Third World people the cost of this would feed…?' she heard Hugo murmuring contemptuously as his fingers touched the soft fabric of her sleeve. His mouth was only centimetres from her own, and Dee knew that merely to breathe would bring it even closer, but she still couldn't resist the urge to verbally defend herself. After all, it wasn't as if he was any less expensively dressed.

'It was a present,' she told him angrily. 'From a friend.'

'A friend...' Hugo's eyebrows rose. 'A *friend*, and not your husband?'

'I don't *have* a husband,' Dee gritted furiously. 'No husband!'

Something hot and dangerous flared in his eyes and Dee started to panic, but it was too late. The damage had already been done, the tinder lit.

'No husband,' Hugo repeated thickly. 'What did he do, Dee? Refuse to play the game your way...just like I did...?'

'No. I—'

Dee gave a gasp and then made a small shocked sound as the pressure of Hugo's mouth on her own prevented her from saying *anything* else.

It had been so long since she had been kissed like this. So long since she had been kissed at all. So long since she had felt... Hungrily her mouth opened under Hugo's, and equally hungrily her hands reached for him.

She was reacting to him as though she was starving for him...dying for him, Dee recognised as she fought to control the primeval flood of her own desire. Her reaction to him must be something to do with all her dredging up of the past, she decided dizzily. It couldn't be because she still wanted him, not after all these years... Years when she had been willingly and easily celibate...years when the *last* thing she had ever imagined herself doing was something like this. He was kissing her properly now, releasing her arms to cup her face.

Dee gave a gasping moan beneath her breath as his tongue traced the shape of her lips. If he kept on kissing her like this... Beneath her sweater she could feel the taut ache in her breasts—an ache that was already spreading wantonly even deeper through her body.

Against her mouth Hugo was saying tauntingly, 'No husband, you say. Well, it certainly shows.'

Immediately Dee came to her senses. Angrily she pushed him away, managing to lever herself off the wall as she did so.

'I've heard the rumours about women of a certain age, with their biological clocks ticking away, but...'

'But you prefer them slightly younger...around Dr Jane's age, no doubt,' was the only reply that Dee's shaking lips could frame.

She was totally stunned by her own behaviour, her own reaction, her own feelings. What on earth had she thought she was doing? She felt as though she had been subjected to a whirlwind which had sprung up out of nowhere, leaving her...devastated.

'What I prefer is...my business,' he told her quietly, and then, whilst she was still trying to pull herself together, he demanded curtly, 'How long have you been divorced?'

'Divorced!' Dee stared at him. 'I'm *not* divorced,' she told him weakly. She saw the look on his face and then added angrily, 'I'm not divorced because I have *never* been married.'

'Not married? But I was told... I heard...' He was frowning at her. 'I heard that you'd married your cousin and that you had a daughter...'

Dee thought quickly. Two of her cousins *had* married, and they *did* have a daughter of nine now, but she didn't tell Hugo so, simply shrugging instead, and informing him dismissively, 'Well, I'm afraid you heard wrong. That's what listening to gossip does for you,' she added pointedly. 'I'm not married, I don't have a daughter, and I'm most certainly not a victim of my biological clock.' Two truths—one fib. But she was determined that Hugo wasn't going to know that!

'You wanted children so much. I can remember that that was one of the things we used to argue about. I wanted us to wait until we'd had a few years together before we started a family, but you were insistent that you wanted a baby almost straight away, just as soon as we were married.'

As he spoke automatically Dee reached for the bare place on her ring finger which had once carried his special ring—a family heirloom he had given her to mark their commitment to one another.

'So that's two things we still have in common,' she said. 'Neither of us is married and neither of us has children.'

'Three things, in fact, when you count...' He was looking at her mouth, Dee recognised, and beneath her sweater the ache in her breasts became an open yearning pulse.

'Three...?' she managed to question croakily, ignoring the savage tug of her own newly awakened sexuality.

'Mmm...both of us are involved in fundraising for charitable organisations. I'd better go up and see Peter,' he added calmly.

'Er, yes…I…' She was behaving as foolishly as though she were still the teenage girl he had knocked off her bicycle as he'd come flying round the corner on his way to one of Peter's meetings—a meeting he had never actually attended. By the time he had picked her up and carefully checked her over for bruises or any other damage, and then insisted on taking her for a restorative cup of coffee, Peter's meeting had been over—but their love affair had just been beginning.

Half an hour later Dee had said goodbye to Peter and was on her way back home. The dazzling sun shining through her windscreen was making her head start to ache—or was her headache being caused by something far more personal?

She still couldn't believe she had reacted the way she had to Hugo's kiss. It was just so totally foreign to her nature to allow herself to get so out of control, never mind to exhibit such naked sexual hunger… How Hugo must have been laughing at her, enjoying her self-inflicted humiliation, enjoying her eager desire for him…her need…

Groaning under her breath, Dee suddenly realised that she was almost in danger of overtaking a car which was in the outside lane of the motorway whilst she was on the inside one, and quickly she took her foot off the accelerator.

She shouldn't be thinking about Hugo. By rights what she ought to be concentrating on was the problems Peter's continuing ill health could cause her professionally. Perhaps now was the time to tactfully find

Hugo had a different relationship with his parents than she'd had with her father. For a start he had two of them, a father *and* a mother, and he had siblings, an older brother and two sisters. And, in the tradition of the British upper classes, he had been sent away to boarding-school, and so, to him, the closeness which had existed between Dee and her father—their mutual dependence on one another, the loyalty and love she'd felt for him—had been hard for him to comprehend.

Hugo...

Dee wrapped her hands defensively around her coffee mug, giving up any attempt now to pretend that she was going to work. It had been such a shock to see him again, but nothing like as much of a shock as it had been when he had kissed her. And yet Hugo and kisses were linked inescapably together in her mind, her memories. The one impossible to detach from the other.

Hugo and kisses...

Dee sat back in her chair and let her mind drift...

CHAPTER FOUR

'Mmm... Just imagine what it would be like to be kissed by that...' Dee's companion murmured appreciatively as she rolled her eyes and cast a slumberously eager glance in Hugo's direction.

'Don't you mean him?' Dee corrected her primly, affecting not to be impressed by the picture of stunning male sensuality that Hugo made, taut muscles rippling down his back and arms as he pulled powerfully on the oars of the boat he was helping to crew.

'Mmm...what I wouldn't give for an hour on my own with him,' her fellow student breathed excitedly, ignoring Dee's disapproving shake of her head.

'Oh, come on,' she protested when Dee refused to relent. 'You can't pretend that you can't see how scrumptiously sexy he is.'

'He's very good-looking,' Dee conceded sedately.

'Good-looking! He's a hundred, million, zillion times more than just good-looking,' Mandy breathed blissfully. 'He's just a living, breathing, walking, talking hunk. He's... Oh, no, he's looking at us. He's looking at us,' she whispered frantically to Dee. 'Dee, he's looking at us...'

'No, he's not; he's squinting because the sun's in his eyes,' Dee corrected her, but for some reason her own heart had given a funny little throb as Hugo had turned his head and appeared to look over in their direction. She knew perfectly well what her companion had meant when she'd tried to find the words to describe Hugo's sexual appeal.

'Lord, but I think I'd die if he ever actually spoke to me. I mean, Hugo Montpelier. *The* man...*the* hunk...*the* dreamboat. He could have any girl he wanted, but he doesn't sleep around and he doesn't have a steady. One of the third years actually tried to ask him out, but he said that he didn't have time and that he was too busy. He's quite definitely hetero, though, no doubt about *that*. One of the girls taking Modern Languages told me that she'd managed to get a snog with him at one of last term's parties and that it was just to die for. She said she practically felt she might have an orgasm there and then, on the spot...'

Dee looked away. Her own sex drive was healthy enough, but her upbringing had been slightly old-fashioned. She had had dates, kissed boys, that kind of thing, and she knew that when she fell in love there would be no holding back from her, but she knew too that her passionate nature meant that she would only feel safe and secure giving herself completely in a relationship if she knew that her feelings were returned. Casual sexual experimentation, playful dabbling in the shallow waters of sexual curiosity were not for her. She was made for the deep, dangerous ocean, the primitive, primal life force of a sexuality that commanded and demanded total commitment from both sides—total commitment and total love.

But that did not mean that she was totally immune to the powerful aura of Hugo Montpelier's strongly male sexuality. He wore it like a banner, proudly and fiercely, and yet at the same time he wore it like a shield, protectively and defensively. Dee had heard all the gossip and speculation about him, the excited girl-chat that went on in the hyped-up, female-hormone-drenched atmosphere of their first-year halls. She had listened to the fevered and feverish uninhibited fantasies of her peers, which ranged from the foolishly idiotic to the frankly obscene.

Less than two months into her first term at university, she might still physically be a virgin but mentally her sexual knowledge had been expanded in a way that quite frankly had left her feeling slightly shocked.

One of the fantasies she had heard expressed regarding Hugo was whether he could last long enough to fully satisfy an excited pair of girls who had graphically described just what they would like to do with him if they had him in bed with them, and just what they would like him to do with them.

'Didn't you know? It's every man's special fantasy,' one girl had purred when she had seen Dee's shocked expression. 'And I should know,' she had added tellingly, grinning at Dee. 'Ask my twin sister. There isn't a man alive who doesn't think that he's got what it takes to satisfy two women at the same time.'

'Nor a woman alive who doesn't *know* that he hasn't,' another girl had muttered sardonically to Dee as she'd overheard the other girl's remark.

Three-in-a-bed romps might be what were in the minds of some of the girls who drooled over Hugo, but so far it seemed that none of them had managed to persuade him to join them. He had been seen es-

corting one girl, but she had simply turned out to be
a friend of a friend and already virtually engaged, and
he had been seen at a drinks party escorting the
daughter of one of the university's Chairs, but she
had since gone to America to finish her education.

'So it's open season on him,' one girl had declared
gleefully. 'And don't forget, whoever gets him, we all
want a full report…'

Dee had left at that point. She wasn't a prude but…
But what? But the images the others' comments had
conjured up in her brain were far too private to be
acknowledged, never mind shared. Not that Hugo was
likely to ask her out. She suspected that she simply
wouldn't be his type. He was so popular, so sought
after, that no doubt when he did date a girl he would
choose one who…who what? Who would make no
bones about the fact that she was quite happy to jump
into bed with him and have sex with him simply for
sex's sake? Whilst she, Dee… No, they would have
nothing in common.

Three days later, as though fate had overheard her
and decided to teach her a lesson, she found out just
how wrong her judgement had been.

There she was, riding her hired bicycle across the
cobbles, struggling to control it, when Hugo came
racing round the side of the building, the full weight
of his body hitting her sideways on.

Neither she nor the cycle had stood any chance. He
was six feet three and a sportsman, she was five feet
nine and slim, the cycle was nearly twenty years old
and rheumaticky; the result was inevitable. Regrettably the cycle, venerably ancient though it was, was

left to fend for itself whilst Hugo went to Dee's rescue.

She was picked up, carefully dusted off, and even more carefully inspected for damage, and all the time Hugo was apologising to her in his deep rough voice that made her feel rather as if a cat was licking her skin with its rough tongue. But his hands as he touched her were anything but rough; he was so careful and tender with her. Her shirt, a neatly buttoned-up affair, had a rip in it and her jeans had dirt stains down one side. The combs had fallen out of her hair and there was a nasty patch of grazing on her index and middle fingers, where they had come into contact with the gravel, but otherwise she was all right—as Dee gravely assured Hugo.

'Thank goodness for that,' he said in relief. 'For a moment I thought I might really have hurt you.'

'It was an accident,' Dee felt bound to point out. It was very chivalrous of him to shoulder all the blame, especially when both of them knew that she shouldn't really have been cycling where she had.

'Look, I was on my way to a meeting, but would you let me buy you a coffee? You never know,' he told her gravely, 'you could be suffering from shock.'

There was no 'could be' about it, Dee admitted inwardly, though her shock wasn't caused by her fall but by the fact that he had actually offered to buy her a coffee, which must mean...

'You *have* hurt yourself,' she heard Hugo saying tersely as he suddenly caught sight of her fingers.

'Oh, my hand—that's nothing,' Dee denied, trying to tuck her grazed fingers out of sight behind her back just in case he decided that their gravel-pitted state meant that she wasn't fit to be seen in a coffee shop.

'Nothing…let me see.'

Before she could stop him he had taken hold of her hand and was gravely inspecting it. Dee wasn't small, and her hands were elegantly long and fine-boned, although when compared with Hugo's they suddenly looked almost deliciously frail and feminine.

Her heart tripping excitedly against her ribs, Dee watched as he carefully brushed away the bits of gravel adhering to her skin.

'This should really be cleaned,' he told her gravely. 'I've got rid of all the gravel, but…'

'It's fine,' Dee started to say, and then stopped, unable to speak, unable to draw breath, unable to do anything as Hugo lifted her fingers to his mouth and slowly and carefully started to suck on them.

Dee felt as though she was going to faint. The sensation was just so unbelievable, the warmth, the wetness, the slow, rhythmic sucking movement of his mouth.

She tried to protest, and managed to make a sound that came out like a small whimper, the merest breath, more easily recognisable as one of intense appreciation than one of protest.

Much later Hugo told her that he hadn't initially meant his action to be sexual. He had simply been genuinely concerned about the state of her hand and had reacted promptly and very much in the fashion of his own practical, prosaic country-bred mother, who had, when he was a small child, often 'cured' small childhood cut fingers and bruises with a cleansing maternal lick.

'All mother animals do it,' he told Dee simply.

'Yes,' she agreed, doe-eyed, 'but you weren't... you aren't my mother.'

'No,' he conceded, 'I'm not your mother.' And then he gently continued with what he had been doing, which was peeling her pretty lace bra away from the fullness of her breasts so that he could expose the dark pink crests to his ardent gaze and even more ardent mouth...

Although the area of the campus they were in when the accident happened was normally a busy one, today, for some unaccountable reason, no one else seemed to be around and they were, to all intents and purposes, alone, so that there was no one else to hear the small anguished sound of shocked virginal pleasure that Dee made, nor the totally male, all-male, all-possessive look that Hugo gave her in response. His gesture might not have begun nor been intended as sexually erotic, but by the time he slowly relinquished her fingers neither of them was in any doubt as to what it was or how it was affecting them—nor what it portended. Peter's meeting—their shared destination—was forgotten.

Dee walked at Hugo's side in a daze as he guided her, guarded her almost, keeping her body protectively and possessively close to his own, towards the café. Her bike he had disposed of, propped up against a wall. She would, no doubt, have to pay a hefty fine to the firm she had rented it from for the damage caused, inflicted on its ancient frame, but Dee didn't care. Quite simply she wasn't capable of caring about anything or anyone right now, and nor was Hugo.

The café Hugo chose was small and dark, smelling richly of fresh ground beans and thick with cigarette smoke. He guided her downstairs to its dimly lit cellar and to a small table tucked away in a natural alcove, his body shielding her from anyone's curious or predatory gaze.

He ordered for them both, a cappuccino for her and a coffee, plain, black and strong, for himself.

'I got used to drinking it like this last summer, when I was doing volunteer work in Africa,' he told her when their coffee arrived.

A simple enough statement, and yet it proved to be both the cornerstone and the basic foundation on which they went on to build their relationship, promoting between them a sense of shared purpose, an intimacy which Dee, with her upbringing, might have found very difficult to reach out for had they taken the route of learning about one another simply through their sexual desire for one another.

Much, much easier for her to let down her guard and express a very natural and enthusiastic interest in his voluntary work than to respond to him or acknowledge her sexual awareness of him. Much easier for her to be herself, to show herself and all the charming complexities of her delicately drawn personality through the questions he then asked her in return than if he had only been able to communicate with her through the guarded protective response she might have made to merely sexual overtures—which was not to say that there was no mental or verbal communication between them; there was, very much so. It surrounded them almost visibly and physically, crating so powerful an aura that the girl bringing them their second and then their third cups of coffee sighed enviously as she went back to the kitchen to tell the girls there about the pair of besotted lovers sitting at one of their tables.

They talked for so long that they missed Peter's meeting completely.

'I don't want to let you go,' Hugo told Dee as they left the coffee shop and stood together on the busy street outside. 'There's so much I want to tell you...so much I want you to tell me. I want to know everything there is to know about you, right from the day you were born.'

Dee laughed, flushed, and then laughed again, before protesting, 'Oh, but that would take all night.' And then she flushed again, but it wasn't embarrassment that was making her skin glow so warmly. It was the way she was feeling inside, just thinking about what it would be like to spend the night with Hugo.

She saw that Hugo was smiling, a male glittery smile that made her heart flip over. It made him look so dangerous, so attractive...so...so...sexy...

'So...?' he whispered.

'I...' Dee felt herself floundering, flustered and incoherent as she fought for some semblance of adult sophistication, some slick answer that would defuse the exciting tension building up between them.

But where another and more experienced girl might have teased, tongue-in-cheek—'so...persuade me'—

all Dee could manage was a stammered, 'I can't... I don't...' She stopped and shook her head, and then told him with honest simplicity, 'I don't do things like that.' She saw his eyes widen before he gave her a swift, comprehensive look that rested on her mouth, her breasts, and then lower, before returning to her eyes.

'What...not ever?' he asked her gruffly.

From somewhere Dee found the courage to meet his eyes and hold his steady look.

'Not ever,' she confirmed.

'The tribe I was working with last summer have a tradition that whilst a girl has to marry a man chosen by her family she has the right to choose for herself the man who will be her first lover. It's considered the greatest honour a woman can bestow on a man, to choose him and to choose him out of love, to bestow on him her love and herself, and I happen to agree.'

Dee could feel herself starting to tremble, while her body had become taut with responsive desire.

'Of course, some of the men get a little bit impatient waiting to be chosen, and then they snatch away the girl of their choice in case she chooses someone else. They seduce her with gifts and kisses.'

His voice was dropping as he spoke to her, becoming lower and raw. Dee made a little husky sound of protest, and as her lips parted Hugo warned her thickly, '*Don't* do that. Otherwise *I* shall be the one stealing *you* away. Have dinner with me tonight,' he begged her abruptly, and then, when she hesitated, he told her, 'You needn't worry. I'm not suggesting...

It will be somewhere safely public,' he told her gravely, 'for both our sakes. The way I feel about you...' He stopped and shook his head.

'In Africa a man considers himself to be very much a man, and his woman very much *his* woman, very, very responsive to *him*, and their love a sacred thing if she conceives his child the first time they make love. Here, in our so-called civilisation, things are different.

'Once you were in my arms I know that I wouldn't be able to stop myself from responding to man's most basic instinctive urge, to bury myself as deep inside you as I could, to give my seed, give our *child* the very best chance it could have of being conceived. And I know, too, that that would be the very worst thing that could happen to it and us right now... I've seen students struggling with domesticity and a baby. It doesn't work,' he told her flatly.

Dee was too shaken by his earlier comments to say anything. Deep down inside her body she could feel her *own* very basic response to *him*, and she knew that what he'd said had touched a deep cord within her.

Of course she didn't want to get pregnant. Of course she didn't. But of course she did—oh, how she did. But she couldn't...wouldn't...

'Do you understand what I'm trying to say to you?' Hugo was asking her tenderly. 'Dinner is all that I can let myself give you tonight, Dee, even though it's very far from all I *want* to give you. Very, very far. So will you, please, please have dinner with me?'

'Yes,' Dee responded simply.

After she left him she made a detour on her way back home to call at her doctor's surgery and ask for an appointment to discuss birth control. She knew she was blushing as she made her request, but the receptionist was completely matter-of-fact about the whole thing.

Dee knew that most of her fellow students were using one form of birth control or another.

'You *can't* leave it up to the men,' one of her house-sharers had commented bluntly as she had hunted in the bathroom for the small white pill she had lost as it popped out of the packet. 'After all, they are *our* bodies, and *we're* the ones who have the right to decide.'

'The right and the responsibility,' another girl had chimed in, a little bitterly. 'The two go hand in hand.'

Hand in hand... Dee looked down at where *her* hand was linked with Hugo's.

To her relief none of the others had been there when he had come to collect her.

'Nice place,' he commented as Dee closed the front door behind them. 'Must be quite pricey to rent, though, even sharing...'

'Not really...and it isn't rented. I'm actually buying it,' Dee told him casually. 'It's a good investment. Dad is helping me. I haven't made my mind up yet, but I may keep it on even when I've finished my degree course. The rental I could get will cover the mortgage and the running costs, and property prices are rising at the moment, so... In fact, I think it could be an idea to buy a few more, but to do that I'd have to ask Dad to let me break into my trust fund and I'm not sure—'

'Your trust fund?' Hugo gave her a sharp look. 'Now you're scaring me. That sounds like pretty serious money.'

Dee stopped walking to look uncertainly at him. She didn't normally speak so unguardedly to people about her personal background, but she felt so relaxed with him, and besides, he had talked about his days at public school and his own background, so she had assumed that his parents were financially well off.

Now it seemed she had been wrong.

'My family is land-rich but money-poor,' he told her dryly, correctly interpreting the questioning uncertainty in her eyes. 'They're rich in family connections and the ability to trace the family tree back to the Norman Conquest. There is money—yes—but it doesn't run to providing each of us with our own private trust funds...'

'Oh, but my father did that because without him I'd be on my own,' Dee protested, anxious to defuse what she feared was going to become a thorny issue between them.

'Yes, I can understand that,' Hugo responded gently. 'If you were mine *I* would want to protect and safeguard you too. I'm just surprised that he allowed you to come to university. From the sound of it I imagine he would have preferred to have you privately educated at home.'

Dee gave him a quick look, warily conscious of the irony beneath the seemingly sympathetic words.

'Perhaps he *is* a little bit old-fashioned,' she responded with quiet dignity, all her protective instincts coming to the fore as she sensed Hugo's unspoken criticism of the father she loved so much. 'But I would much rather have a father like that—a father I can look up to and admire…and trust, a man of…of compassion and…and honour…of integrity—than someone…'

Her voice became suspended with emotion at the thought that she and Hugo might already be on the verge of a quarrel, but immediately Hugo soothed her, gently stroking her hand as he apologised. 'I'm sorry… I shouldn't have implied… I guess I'm just jealous…' he told her whimsically. 'And not just of your trust fund…'

Of course that made her laugh, as he had intended it would, and she was secretly pleased he kept on holding her hand as they walked down the street together.

He hadn't said exactly where they were going, but Lexminster was a relatively compact city, and after the revelation about her trust fund she was reluctant to suggest that they could take her car to their destination.

Later, when she discovered the cavalier attitude Hugo had to driving—he had learned to drive in an ancient Land Rover on his grandfather's estate and further honed his 'skill' driving across the dry, mud-scarred ribbed and ridged empty riverbeds of the drought-ridden area where he had done his voluntary work—she would be glad she had not been subjected to it on their first date.

It was a late November evening, with just a warning that frost might be in the air later. The autumn had been fine and dry, and the leaves were still at the delicious stage of rustling pleasurably beneath one's feet when walked on, their scent evocative and slightly pungent on the clear air as they walked down the tree-lined main street of the city.

The restaurant Hugo had chosen was a small Italian family-run place, down a narrow side street, and Dee fell in love with it and the family who owned and ran it the moment they walked in.

They greeted Hugo like a member of the family, Luigi, the burly grey-haired patron, punching him genially on the shoulder and then wincing in mock pain and shaking his arm.

'He is built like an ox…like a bull,' he amended, with a laughing look in Dee's direction.

Of course she blushed, and of course Bella, his wife, tutted and protested that Luigi was embarrassing her, smothering Dee with warmly maternal concern and protection as she assured her that she was not to take any notice of Luigi's poor attempt at humour.

'What? You mean to say that you do *not* think of me as a bull?' Hugo teased Bella, lifting his arm and tensing his muscles in a mock display of male strength.

'Aha, it is not the size of this muscle *here* that counts,' Luigi warned him. 'Is that not so, *cara*?' he asked his outraged wife.

Dee listened to their byplay with a mixture of delight and self-consciousness. Luigi was barely her own height, and Bella was even smaller, both of them plump and round and very obviously well and happily married. So much so that it was impossible for Dee to take offence at Luigi's references to Hugo's sexual machismo. He was as proud of him as though Hugo had been his own son, as proud of Hugo's maleness as though it had been his own, and it was a simple and honest pride, with nothing offensive or prurient about it.

'She is *bella*, very *bella*,' he told Hugo approvingly, after he had subjected Dee to a thorough and very malely appreciative visual inspection, his eyes twinkling as he made this report to Hugo.

'She is indeed, and she is *my bella*,' Hugo retorted warningly.

It was the start of one of the most magical evenings of Dee's life.

She ate and drank with an appetite that was totally unfamiliar to her. Hugo, she noticed, whilst he enjoyed his food and his wine, was careful not to drink too much nor to allow her to do so, and she acknowledged that she loved his protective attitude towards her. It made her feel so...so safe, so cherished...so loved.

So loved.

There was no doubt in Dee's mind that she was in love. She had been in love from the moment Hugo had picked her up off the gravel, she suspected, and it was the most intoxicating, the most exciting, the most life-enhancing emotion she had *ever* experienced.

It was late when they left the restaurant. The promised frost had become reality, sparkling on the ground and the trees, vaporising their breath as Dee gave a small gasp at the cold shock of it against her face.

'It's so cold,' she protested as she huddled deeper into her coat.

'Mmm... Come here, then,' Hugo told her, wrapping his arm around her as he drew her as close as he could to his own body.

Happily nestling close to him, Dee laughed when he tucked his hand into her pocket.

'Aha...all you *really* wanted to do was to keep your hand warm in my pocket,' she teased him.

'Wrong,' Hugo corrected her huskily. 'All I *really* want to do is to keep *all* of you warm in my bed, with my body...my hands and my mouth. Has anyone ever made any kind of love to you, Dee? Has anyone ever touched you...kissed you...?'

'Of course they have,' she squeaked indignantly. Just because she was a virgin that didn't mean she was *totally* sexually ignorant.

'In my last year at school I went to loads of snogging parties...'

She could see the little puffs of white air appearing from Hugo's mouth as his body gusted with laughter.

'Oh, snogging parties... That wasn't *exactly* the kind of kissing I meant. What I meant was, has anyone kissed you...intimately, caressed your body with their mouth, explored you with their hands and their tongue, made you...?'

Frantically Dee covered her ears, torn between excited shock and self-conscious chagrin that he had to explain to her so graphically just what he meant. She knew what he was describing, of course, had even wondered in her most private intimate moments just how it would feel to have a man, *her* man, make love to her in such a way, but she had never dreamed that she would walk down a public street whilst he, that man, teasingly described to her an act which she had assumed was something a man only did for a woman if she was very, very fortunate or very, very loved.

'Do I take it that that's a no?' Hugo asked her, still laughing, but Dee could hear the rusty betraying note in his voice, and she could see the way he was looking at her. She might not be sexually experienced, but she was no fool. Hugo wanted to touch her, caress her, taste her, in the way he had just described, and unless she had got it wrong he wanted to do it very, very badly indeed and very, very soon…like now, in fact. Her heart started to thud. She felt dizzy with excitement and the euphoria-inducing realisation of her own female power.

'Oh, it's going to be so good for us,' Hugo groaned as he drew her into the shadow of a convenient side street and swept her promptly and expertly into his arms. Not that Dee was attempting very much resistance, and she didn't offer any either a few seconds later, when he slipped his hands inside her coat and wrapped his arms around her body so tightly she felt she could hardly breathe. Their kiss was everything that a first kiss should be—tender, exciting, passionate, their mouths eager and hungry, their bodies urgently hungry for the feel of the other. But even though Hugo had put his hands under her coat, a little to Dee's surprise he made no attempt to do anything more than simply hold her.

'I daren't,' he told her gruffly, his voice muffled between kisses as though he could read what she was thinking. 'God knows I want to, but if I touch you now... Remember what I said to you this afternoon?'

'About...about making babies...' Dee responded shakily.

'Don't. Don't even say it,' Hugo groaned as he moved his body even closer to her own, swiftly unfastening his own coat. Dee could feel his hard arousal. Immediately her own body quickened, revealing a capacity for sexual responsiveness which she had never guessed she possessed. The nature and the intensity of the ache raging through her shocked her, and yet it excited her as well.

Her fellow students' lusty comments about sharing their beds and their bodies with Hugo slipped warningly into her mind, and instantly she was seized with such a strong surge of female determination and possessive jealousy at the thought of someone daring to try to take away her man that the primitiveness of her emotions bemused her.

'What is it...? What's wrong?' Hugo asked her. He had buttoned up her coat and was smiling tenderly down at her as his hand cupped her face, and his forefinger firmly tilted her face up to his so that he could look into her eyes.

'I was just thinking about something one of the other girls said and how jealous it was making me,' Dee responded honestly.

'What girl?' Hugo asked her, puzzled. 'There is no girl, and I promise you,' he added, his voice dropping huskily, 'I shall never give you any cause to be jealous. I would never, could never, do anything to hurt you. There is no other girl.'

'No,' Dee agreed, smiling up at him. But she still couldn't resist murmuring mischievously, 'Still, I'm glad that *I* don't have a twin sister...'

'What?'

She laughed and shook her head, refusing to explain. There was no way she would *ever* want to share Hugo with another woman, in bed or out of it. No way at all.

CHAPTER FIVE

THEY had been going out together for over a month before they finally made love, although Dee knew that no one who saw them together during those early weeks would have believed it.

Dee hadn't said anything about either her running into Hugo or having dinner with him to any of her friends, but within a week, in the way that these things so often had of getting out, it seemed that everyone did know.

It was only later that Hugo actually admitted that he had let it be known that she was his.

'I had to do it. Just in case anyone else started to make a play for you,' he defended himself.

Dee shook her head, but by then she was too much in love, too deeply committed to him to protest very much. Those were heady days, exciting days, frustrating days too. Her doctor had warned her that it would be several weeks before she could rely completely on the efficiency of her birth control pill to prevent an unwanted pregnancy, and Hugo had announced very firmly that there was no way he wanted them to run that risk. He also wanted there to be nothing between them the first time they made love together. 'And I mean *nothing*,' he had repeated, with heavy sensual emphasis.

Both of them had family commitments which

74

would take them home and away from each other over Christmas. Hugo was going north with his parents, to spend Christmas and the New Year with his grandfather.

'A huge quarrelsome gathering of our clan—quite literally,' he told Dee wryly. 'My grandfather insists that we stick to tradition, despite the fact that Montpelier House is a huge great freezing barn of a place that's impossible to heat. My parents will have a row on the journey up there because my mother won't want to go, and another on the way back because my father won't want to leave. It happens every year. My elder sister's children will cause complete havoc and chaos, and my younger sister, who doesn't have any, will get all high-minded and sanctimonious about the way she is bringing them up, insisting that she's spoiling them, and then they'll both turn on me when I tell them not to be such idiots... I promise you, it's dreadful.'

'It sounds wonderful,' Dee told him enviously. She too would be spending Christmas with her own extended family. She and her father would be visiting the farm where he had been brought up and which was now farmed by his brother. Dee's cousins would be there, and her aunts and uncles, and there was a good-sized group of them, but Dee and her father had always been a little on the outside of everything. Her father was something of an enigma to the rest of his family, and, whilst they loved him, they never seemed to feel totally at home or relaxed in his company, Dee had noticed, and that had rubbed off on her too.

'My brother has more in common with his livestock than he has with me,' her father had once commented witheringly to her after a particularly sharp exchange between the two men. There would be jokes and party games at the farm, but Dee knew that she would not be able to throw herself into it as unselfconsciously as she would have liked because she'd be conscious of the fact that her father could not do so.

The best bit of Christmas for her had always been the quiet shared hours she and her father spent alone together: the ritual attendance at church, the early-morning rising, the excitement as a child of her stocking, the comfort of the traditional cooked breakfast after their return from church, followed by the thrill of opening her proper presents. These days the present bit of Christmas was, of course, not quite so exciting, but she still enjoyed their small traditions.

Her father was a keen swimmer. As a young man he had swum for the county, and this year Dee had been thrilled to find a book in Lexminster by one of his boyhood heros, a little-known Channel swimmer, which she knew he would be delighted to have. He also had a weakness for Turkish delight, which she had also bought him, and she had saved hard for an antique snuff box to add to his extensive collection.

He would, she knew, give her a small parcel of shares—a gift and a test, for she was free to do what she wished with them, either keep them or sell them. All she had to do was use her own judgement to decide. The shares would be in unfamiliar companies: Australian mines, South American crops. Last year she had been spectacularly successful in her decision. The shares she had kept had increased their value two hundredfold. She would be hard put to it to better that this year.

She missed Hugo, as she had known she would. After all, they had been seeing each other every day, and she was so very, very much in love with him— and he with her. What she hadn't expected or been totally prepared for was the way his absence manifested itself in an actual physical ache of longing for him.

Her father guessed that something was wrong, and Dee could hear the curt note of disapproval in his voice as he demanded to know, 'What's wrong with you, Dee? I hope you haven't done anything foolish and got involved with some student...'

Hugo isn't 'some student,' Daddy, Dee wanted to protest, but something stopped her, warning her that her father wasn't quite ready yet to admit another man into her life or her heart. In the last few weeks she had become far more aware of the vulnerability of the male ego. After all, Hugo could, at times, display an unexpected vein of jealousy against her father which both touched and amused her, making her feel so protectively tender towards them both that it made her heart ache.

'He's my father and you're my...you're mine,' she had whispered reassuringly to him as she'd lain in his arms.

They had been at his flat, untidy and strewn with papers and possessions. It even smelt different from her own all-female household, Dee recognised. Although they still hadn't actually made love in the fullest sense of the words, there was very little that Hugo did not know about her body, nor her about his. It had shocked her a little to discover how easily and thoroughly he could satisfy her and she him without that final act of penetration, but that did not mean that she did not want it.

Looking lovingly up into his eyes, she had teased the thick springy curls of his hair with her fingers. She loved the way it brushed his shoulder and her own skin when he kissed and caressed it. It felt so soft and yet so strong...so vibrant...just like him. She liked to bury her face in it and breathe in its scent, *his* scent. It suited him worn that length, made him look individual, gave him all the romantic appeal of a macho Renaissance warrior knight...

They did, of course, speak to one another often over the Christmas holiday, and then, three days before they had arranged that they would go back to Lexminster, Hugo rang her.

'I can't bear it any longer,' he groaned passionately. 'I've got to see you.'

'But it's too soon. We said next Monday, and besides, you're in the north and—'

'No, I'm not, I'm here...back...'

'In Lexminster?' Dee gasped. 'But...'

'You can come to me, Dee,' he told her softly. 'Or I can come and get you... I don't mind which, but I can't spend another night without seeing you.'

He could come and get her. Dee could just imagine her father's reaction to that!

As it was it was difficult enough convincing him that she needed to return to university three days ahead of the time she had already stipulated. He was

t from these,' he agreed, putting down his glass.
I tell you how I intend to drink it?' he whis-
as he came towards her and removed her own
before taking her in his arms. 'I intend to pour
your naked body and lick every droplet off
rink every last bubble, and then I shall...'
should have sounded ridiculous, but somehow
n't; somehow she was reacting to what he was
, the picture he was drawing in her mind and
senses, with a frantic little shudder that made
oan and start to kiss her with uninhibited pas-

had just started to unfasten her top when they
he door. Cursing, he released her and went to
. It was the waiter with their supper, and Dee
hat as he wheeled in the table her face was as
her champagne. The meal Hugo had chosen
erything that a romantic meal should be. Dee
't imagine how much it must have cost him.
, her favourite tiny wild strawberries, hand-
hocolates, the kind he knew she had a passion
of it washed down by carefully chosen wine—
Dee only sipped at hers. Hugo, she noticed,
same.
sfied?' Hugo asked her softly, when Dee had
he last of the chocolate truffles.
colour rose, but Dee still managed to meet his
she told him boldly, 'No, and I shan't be

l...?' Hugo pressed as she stopped speaking.
l I can feel you inside me,' she whispered on
n rush, but now she couldn't quite manage to

huffy and a little distant with her, and Dee knew why, even though she tried to pretend that she was not aware of his reaction. No mention was made of Hugo, and Dee cravenly hoped that there would not be...not yet...not whilst their feelings for one another were so...so overpoweringly intense. She wasn't ready yet to let anyone else into their relationship, not even someone as close as her father.

As she drove away from him, for the first time in her life Dee knew that she was actually happy to leave her father behind. She loved him dearly, of course she did, but now there was a new male focus in her life; now she was ready to step from girlhood into womanhood, from the protection of her father's arms to the excitement of Hugo's. She had rung him to tell him that she was leaving and he was waiting for her when she arrived.

'Don't get out of the car,' he told her as he hurried down the stone steps leading to her house, where he had been sheltering from the driving rain.

'*Don't* get out? But I thought you wanted...'

'Oh, I do, I do,' he assured her wickedly, with a sabre-toothed male smile. 'But not here...'

'Not here? But...'

'I want this to be special...very, very special,' he told her huskily, and then he urged her, 'I'll drive you...'

'No, I'll drive,' Dee told him firmly. 'Where are we going?'

When he told her she gasped.

'You've booked us a room at the De Villiers Hotel—but, Hugo, that will cost a fortune.'

'No, not a room,' he contradicted her.

Dee looked at him. She knew his zany sense of humour by now.

'Not a room... What, then? A wooden seat in the grounds?' she asked warily.

'No, not that.' Hugo laughed. 'I've booked us a suite,' he told her quietly.

'A suite...' Dee squeaked. 'But Hugo, the cost...'

'Mmm...I know; I hope I'm going to be worth it,' he told her, straight-faced, making her dissolve into giggles.

The hotel wasn't very far away, just a few miles the other side of the city, a beautiful Edwardian house set in its own grounds which had been converted to a very prestigious hotel. Dee had been there once—with her father, when he had taken her out for a birthday lunch. The food, the room, the service had all been first-class, and Dee had felt truly spoiled and treasured.

It was a favourite with local brides, not for their receptions so much as for their wedding nights. Rumour had it that the discreet addition of a Jacuzzi to the bridal suite had resulted in totally blissed-out couples pronouncing fervently that they were most definitely going to come back.

At the thought of the bridal suite and its Jacuzzi Dee suddenly felt very hot, and slightly dizzy.

'You haven't...it isn't...you haven't booked the bridal suite, have you?' she asked Hugo faintly.

He laughed again.

'No, I haven't,' he reassured her, adding, tongue-

in-cheek, 'We don't want everyo[ne] we're going to be doing, do we?'

'You mean to say they won't [   ] dryly.

He hadn't booked the bridal suit[e   ] neglected to tell her was that *all* [   ] suites possessed their own Jacuzzi[s   ]

As Hugo told Dee later, he just [   ] a camera for that unforgettable lo[ok   ] the porter swept into the room an[d   ] door to the large *en suite* bathroo[m   ] flourish.

'How could you?' she whispere[d   ] porter had gone. 'It makes me fee[l   ] so...so obvious.'

'One of us certainly is,' Hugo ag[reed   ] glance down at his own body.

Dee closed her eyes. She gave [   ] you do with such a man?

Hugo soon showed her, adroitly [   ] and then going over to uncork th[e cham-] pagne that was chilling in an ice b[ucket   ]

'I've ordered us a cold supper,' [   ] first...' He poured her a glass o[f   ] handed it to her. 'To us...' he toas[ted   ]

A little shakily Dee lifted her gl[ass   ] took a sip. Suddenly, and totally un[   ] side her excitement she could feel [   ] thread of shy, virginal self-consc[ious   ] knowledged.

'We'll never drink all that,' she t[old   ] ily, looking at the large bottle.

sustain that eye-to-eye contact. Not that she needed to. Hugo had already left his seat and was swooping down on her, practically lifting her off her chair as he took her in his arms.

'Oh God, Dee, you don't know what you're doing to me,' he told her rawly, and as she felt the emotion surging through his body Dee realised properly, for the first time, just what a strain the last few weeks must have been for him, and just how much control he must have been exercising over his own desires and needs.

'Come here. Come *here*,' he whispered urgently to her, even though she was already there in his arms, and his words were a soft chant of tender love as he cupped her face and started to kiss her. 'Mmm… You taste of chocolate,' he murmured appreciatively as he tasted her mouth, testing her reaction.

'And you taste of—' She started to tease back, then stopped, her eyes darkening with a passion she made no attempt to hide as she told him huskily, 'And you taste of you, Hugo, and it's the best taste in the world…the *only* taste I could ever want. You are the only man I could ever want, and I want you so badly. I want to touch you, hold you, taste you…'

She heard him groan deep down in his throat, a male purr of tormented longing. She lifted her fingers to his throat and touched it, feeling the vibration of the noise he was making against her fingertips. She loved the feel of his skin, the feel of his body. She loved it when she closed her hand, her *hands*, around him and felt the satisfying hard swell of his body as he reacted to her touch.

'Both hands?' he had teased her, the first time she had wrapped them lovingly around him.

'Mmm…but you do wonders for my ego. *One* will do, Dee…'

'One will *do*,' she had acknowledged. 'But it feels so good to hold you like this, with two…'

'I can't argue with that,' he had agreed throatily, but he had still been laughing a little at her.

He had stopped laughing, though, when she had held him still and bent her head to place a ring of shyly adoring kisses around the taut head of his erection.

Oh, yes, he had stopped laughing then.

Now, with the lights turned down low over the large, luxurious bed, Hugo undressed her slowly. They had been to bed together before, but this time, somehow, it was different…special…and the moment he stepped away from her he gave her a look so full of import that it made Dee shiver a little to read the message in his eyes. This was their night of commitment to one another, the final bridge to cross on their way to *complete* commitment, the final act which they had not yet shared.

They already knew one another's dreams and one another's hopes, they already knew what they were destined to be and to do—that together they would work for the benefit of mankind, that they would leave university to work together in the field, would marry before they left. Hugo was so idealistic—even more so, in some ways, than she was herself. He believed passionately in what he wanted to do and he was totally and utterly committed to it. To deny him the opportunity would be like cutting off one of his limbs, only worse.

'There's so much we can give them, so much we can put back into a culture, a country, that in the past we've only taken from and destroyed, and there's so much we can learn from them. They have so little in materialistic terms, but they have their pride and their dignity—their heritage.

'My father doesn't approve of what I'm planning to do, you know, and neither does my grandfather, but it's something I *have* to do...I couldn't live with myself if I didn't,' he had told her passionately, and Dee had known exactly what he meant. His idealism only made her love him more, even whilst she knew that it would also mean that there would always be a small part of his heart and his emotions that did not belong totally to her.

He was very like *her* father, in that his pride in his own beliefs ran very strongly in him. *Very* like her father.

'It's your turn,' Hugo whispered to her now, as his tender glance caressed and reassured her. Very carefully Dee started to undress *him*, her fingers trembling not with nervousness but with the intensity of her suppressed and aching longing for him.

'No, that's cheating,' she protested huskily when, without waiting for her to finish, he leaned forward and started to nibble the side of her neck, his hand cupping and stroking her naked breast. Dee closed her eyes as she felt her body's reaction, going still as she tried to stem the fierce hot tide of it, rising not so much up through her body as washing fiercely down through it, to that place where the sheer pressure of it forced into life a fierce, tumultuously beating pulse.

Hugo's lips caressed her shoulder, her collarbone, and then moved lower, nuzzling at the soft curve of her breast and then the taut crest of her nipple before closing over that nipple itself. Dee made a fiercely guttural noise of throaty excitement, her fingernails digging into Hugo's skin, but if he felt any pain he certainly didn't show it. However, his slow, careful suckling on her nipple did, suddenly becoming an urgent, body-trembling erotic tug that made Dee groan as she buried her hands in his hair and held him passionately to her.

Somehow she was on the bed. Somehow Hugo was undressed. Somehow he had positioned her so that he could kneel between her splayed legs as he kissed her quivering belly. Now, with no need to control her longing for him, Dee could respond to him as she had so much longed to do, arching her spine and lifting herself to the tormenting lap of his tongue as he licked at the moist slickness of her body. There was no need for the champagne—her own desire had covered her skin in its own sweetly scented mist of arousal—but, wonderful though the touch of his mouth against her body was, it wasn't what Dee really wanted. Not now. Not this time.

'Are you sure you're ready for me? Do you want...?' Hugo asked her hoarsely as she reached for him, wildly begging him, eagerly demanding to feel him deep inside her.

'Oh, yes, yes...' Dee groaned longingly.

She couldn't take her eyes off him, watching him as urgently, as hungrily as he watched her.

'I'm afraid of hurting you,' he confessed as he hesitated, but his body wasn't afraid, Dee recognised, her eyes widening as she watched him lowering himself towards her. He looked so good, so…so ready…so—

She gave a little whimper of sound as she felt him rubbing himself slowly against her.

'That hurt?' Hugo asked her in concern.

Dee managed to laugh.

'Yes,' she told him. 'It hurts because it's not…because I want you *inside* me…' She gave a smothered gasp as she felt the first of the deep penetrative strokes she had so longed for, her eyes widening as she realised how well their bodies fitted together.

No way did the sensation she had of being filled, stretched completely, in *any* way approximate to any kind of pain, but the intensity of her pleasure was so acute that it could almost be described as a kind of special agony, a racking urgency, a pulsing, heart-jerking, driven compulsion that had her calling out Hugo's name as she clung frantically to him.

It didn't last long; both of them were too aroused, too wrought up emotionally and physically, for it to do so. Dee knew she had been virtually on the point of orgasm even before Hugo had entered her, and he had been almost as close to the edge of his own self-control.

Dee had barely felt the first quivering explosion of her own completion when Hugo cried out her name, the hot, fierce pulse of his ejaculation drenching her body with a fiercely sweet burst of pleasure.

She was, Dee discovered seconds later as she relaxed into his arms, crooning happily in delighted pleasure, making soft cooing sounds of love to Hugo as he held her.

'It will be better next time,' she heard him promising her as he smoothed back her hair and kissed her tenderly. 'I'll make it last longer and—'

'*Better*...than *that*...*impossible*!' Dee assured him blissfully.

'Oh, Dee, Dee, is it any wonder that I love you so much?' Hugo praised her adoringly. 'I should not have met you, you know. You shouldn't really have existed. I didn't *plan* for this to happen. I wasn't *going* to fall in love, and I certainly didn't want to make the kind of lifetime commitment I want to make to you to any woman until I was at least thirty.

'It's just as well that you and I share the same ideals and the same ambitions. I don't think I could have borne it if you'd been the kind of woman who expected me to stay at home and get myself the sort of job my father wants me to get. Something in the City that will make me a lot of money. I'm not going to be much of a catch as a husband, you do realise that, don't you? Our children will complain and all your friends will think that you're crazy to love me. Your father will quite definitely disapprove...'

'No, he won't,' Dee denied. 'He'll admire you for what you're doing—and it is admirable, Hugo, to want to help others. I couldn't love you so much as I do if you were any way different from the way you are, and I certainly wouldn't want to change you or the plans you've made.'

'Mmm...it's providential, isn't it, that you'll have completed your degree course just about the same time as I finish my Ph.D.? There's no way I can make time to go back to working in the field until I finish it, but once I have, once we've both completed our studies... There's so much I want to do, Dee. So very, very much...'

'Mmm...I know,' she agreed, and then added with sweet provocativeness, 'You haven't even touched the champagne, and then there's the Jacuzzi... How long have you booked the suite for?'

'Just tonight,' Hugo told her ruefully.

'*Just* tonight? You mean we've still got it for a whole twelve hours?' Dee teased him, mock wide-eyed.

'A whole twelve hours,' he agreed, but he was mumbling the words a little because Dee was kissing him.

'Then we don't have a *moment* to waste, do we?' she told him as she trailed her fingers slowly over his body.

'No, I don't suppose we do,' he agreed.

CHAPTER SIX

DEE woke up with a start. Her heart was pounding and her mouth felt dry. She had slept heavily but not refreshingly, almost as though she had been drugged, and as she lay in bed she was conscious of an unfamiliar reluctance to get up, almost a *dread* of doing so, as though by remaining where she was she could hold her apprehensions and low spirits at bay.

Unfamiliar? Not exactly. Not totally. There had been a period after her father's death, a time once the urgency of the immediate calls upon her time and attention had slackened a little, when she had experienced a similar longing to crawl away and hide somewhere safe and womb-like. She had had to fight to overcome it, to tell herself that the decisions she had made had been right and necessary, to urge herself to go on. Resolutely she threw back the bedclothes and slid her feet to the bedroom floor.

Her bedroom was her own secret, special place, somewhere that no one else was allowed to enter. Not so much because it was a private sanctuary, Dee recognised, but because of what she knew it betrayed about a deeply personal side of her nature.

The walls were painted a soft washed colour, somewhere between blue and green, and the windows were draped in gossamer folds of creamy white muslin. The same fabric fell from the ceiling and was gathered back softly at either side of her double bed, which, like the chaise longue at its foot and the comfortable bedroom chair by the window, was covered in a cream-coloured cotton brocade. The carpet too was cream. The whole ambience of the room was one of soft delicacy. A stranger looking into Dee's bedroom and making a character assessment of her from it would have judged her to be soft and ethereal, a creature of fluid, feminine moods and feelings, a dreamy water sprite of a woman, whose sensibilities were as delicate and tender as the petals of the fresh cream flowers that filled the bowl on the pretty antique table she used as a dressing table.

As Dee showered and then dressed she acknowledged that the cause of her sense of wanting to curl up protectively and let the world get on without her for a while were the two completely contradictory forces lining up against one another for battle inside her head.

On the one side was her need to persuade Peter, without either alienating him or even more importantly hurting him, that it was time for him to step down from the foundation committee, and her knowledge that the best way to achieve that goal would be to win Hugo's support, to actively *court* his help and approval of her plans, whilst on the other was her totally opposing need to have nothing whatsoever to do with him, to blot him completely out of her thoughts, her mind, her life, her heart.

Abruptly Dee stopped brushing her hair, her body convulsing in a small involuntary shiver.

She had fought that battle once, fought it and, she

had believed, won it, inch by painful inch, hour by agonising hour. She put down her hairbrush and stared unseeingly into her mirror. She was afraid, she acknowledged grimly. Afraid of having to re-enter the long, painful time of darkness she had already been through once, afraid of what might happen to her if she allowed Hugo to come back into even the smallest corner of her life, and that was why she had been so reluctant to face the day.

Yes, she was stronger now than the girl she had once been, but then she had had the advantage of being motivated, driven by what she had considered to be almost a crusade; then she had had zeal and youth on her side. Now...

Now she still believed as firmly as she had done then that she had made the right, the only decision, but now the brightness of her fervour, her belief was shadowed, obscured sometimes by her own inner images of what might have been, the child or children she might have had, the life, the love she might have shared.

As a young man Hugo had been, if anything, even more fervent in his beliefs than she had been herself, and, unlike her, he had been sharply critical of what he had termed the selfishness of a materialistic society and those who supported it. As an idealist, his views had sometimes been diametrically opposed to those of her father—or so it had seemed at times.

'What do you expect my father to do?' she had demanded angrily of him once in the middle of one of their passionate arguments. 'Give *all* his money away...?'

'Don't be ridiculous,' Hugo had snorted angrily, in defence of his own beliefs.

He had been equally passionate about how important it was for those involved in aid programmes to be completely free of even the faintest breath of scandal, of anything that could reflect badly on the cause they were representing. Oddly enough, that had been a belief he had actually *shared* with her father.

Perhaps because she was a woman, Dee was inclined to take a more reasonable and compassionate view. Human beings were, after all, human, vulnerable, *fallible*.

There was no point in giving in to her present feelings. She would, she decided firmly, take the bull by the horns and drive over to Lexminster so that she could both see how Peter was and either talk with Hugo or arrange a meeting with him so that she could raise the subject of the committee with him.

Her mind made up, Dee told herself that she had made the right decision. What had happened... existed...between her and Hugo all those years ago had no relevance to her life now, and it certainly had none to his. Her best plan was simply to behave as though they had been no more than mere acquaintances, and to adopt a casually friendly but firmly distancing attitude towards him.

A very sensible decision, but one which surely did not necessitate four changes of clothes and a bedroom strewn with discarded, rejected outfits before Dee was finally ready to set out for Lexminster—over an hour later than she had originally planned.

Even so, it had been worth taking time and trouble

with her appearance, she told herself stoutly as she climbed into her car. Her father had been of the old school, and had firmly believed in the importance of creating the right impression, and in taking time over her clothes she was just acting on those beliefs, Dee assured herself.

The cream dress she was wearing was simple, and the long slits which ran down both sides made it easy to move in without being in any way provocative— at least that was what Dee thought. A man, though, could have told her that there was something quite definitely very deliciously alluring about the discreetly subtle flash of long leg that her skirt revealed when she walked.

Its boat-shaped neckline was sensible—even if, regrettably, it did have an annoying tendency to slide down off one shoulder occasionally—and the little suedette pumps she was wearing with it were similarly 'sensible.' The pretty gold earrings had been a present from her father, and were therefore of sentimental importance, and if she had dashed back into the house just to add a spray of her favourite perfume and check her lipstick—so what?

As Dee drove through the town centre she noticed a small group of teenage boys standing aimlessly in the square, and she started to frown. She knew from the headmaster of the local school, who was on the board of one of her charities, that they were experiencing a growing problem with truancy amongst some of the teenage children.

Ted Richards felt, like her, that the town's teenagers needed a healthy outlet for their energies and, per-

haps even more importantly, that they needed to have
their growing maturity recognised and to feel that
they were a valued part of their own community.

In contrast to the disquieting boredom Dee had recognised in the slouched shoulders and aimless scuf-
fling of the youngsters, when she drove past her own
offices the area outside it was busy, with the town's
senior citizens making use of the comfortable facili-
ties of the coffee shop and meeting rooms on the
ground floor of the building. Only the other morning,
as she had walked through the coffee shop, she had
noticed that the list pinned up on the noticeboard inviting people to join one of the several trips that were
being planned was very fully subscribed.

Teenagers did not always take too enthusiastically
to being over-organised, especially by adults. Dee
knew that, but she was still very conscious of the fact
that their welfare and their happiness was an area
which needed an awful lot of input.

Anna's husband, Ward, had certainly opened her
eyes and inspired her in that regard. Perhaps it might
be worthwhile asking Ward if he would show Peter
round his own workshops, Dee mused as she left the
town behind her—always providing, of course, that
Peter was well enough for such an outing.

Peter had a very special place in Dee's heart. She
never found it boring listening to his stories of his
young manhood, especially when those stories involved her own father.

It was lunchtime when Dee reached Lexminster. In
addition to the file she was compiling containing her
plans for Rye's teenagers, she had also placed in the

boot of her car one of her home-made pies, which were a special favourite of Peter's, as well as some other food.

She had a key for Peter's house, but, out of habit, she automatically knocked on the door first and then, when there was no response, fished the key out of her bag and let herself in, calling out a little anxiously as she stepped into the hallway,

'Peter, it's me—Dee.'

She was just about to head for the kitchen with her groceries when, unexpectedly, the kitchen door opened. But it wasn't Peter who opened it, and as she saw Hugo frowning at her Dee's heart gave a dangerous flurried series of painful little thuds.

'Oh…' Dee's hand went protectively to her throat. 'I didn't… You…'

'I heard you knock but I was on the phone,' Hugo told her curtly before adding, 'Peter's asleep. The doctor was anxious that he should have some proper rest, so she has given him a shot of something to help him sleep.' He frowned as he looked at her disapprovingly. 'I just hope that you haven't woken him.'

To her chagrin his criticism made Dee feel as awkward and guilty as a little girl, causing her to retaliate defensively, 'Was it really necessary or wise of the doctor to drug him?'

'Drug him…what exactly are you implying?'

'I'm not implying anything,' Dee denied. 'But at Peter's age, the fact—'

'Jane is a qualified doctor, Dee, and if she thinks that some mild form of gentle sedation is called for…'

a problem; there's no time limit... My work
ns that I can base myself virtually anywhere just
ong as I have access to the conveniences of mod-
technology.... No...I haven't told her yet, but I
d to do so...'

ee hadn't deliberately eavesdropped on his con-
ation, but it was impossible for her not to have
heard it, even though she had walked into the
As she heard Hugo replacing the receiver, Dee
ed back towards the kitchen.

ince I can't see or speak with Peter, there isn't
h point in my staying. When he does wake up
se give him my love. I've brought some food
—'

e stopped as Hugo cut her off abruptly, telling
orusquely, 'You can't go yet. There's something
e to tell you.'

mething he *had* to tell her? Whatever it was she
l tell from his expression that it wasn't anything
ant. Her heart started to thump. Had Peter said
thing to him about her father...about the past?
no, Peter didn't know. She had never... But he
l have guessed, had his own suspicions...and...
Vhat is it? Tell me...'

e could hear the anxiety crackling in her own
, making it sound harsh.

'e'll go into the other room,' Hugo suggested.
re right under Peter's bedroom here, and I don't
to disturb him.'

r heart pounding in heavy sledgehammer blows,
followed him into the parlour.

e air in the room was stale and stuffy, and au-

Dee's heart twisted betrayingly ov
mate use of the doctor's Christian nar
his voice had softened noticeably as

'I actually needed to talk to Peter,'
deliberately changing the subject. 'B
sedated…'

'You *needed* to talk to him? So th
social visit to enquire after his health
pounced.

'I *am* concerned about his health, of

'But obviously not concerned eno
called in a doctor,' Hugo pointed out d

Dee could feel her face starting to bur
ture of guilt and anger.

'I *would* have done so, but, as I expl
day, I haven't—'

'Had time. Yes, I know. What was it
to talk to Peter about?'

Dee looked sharply at him. There wa
could bring herself to enlist Hugo's aid
being so antagonistic towards her.

'I rather think that that is Peter's and
don't you?' she asked him coolly.

Immediately Hugo's eyebrows rose
was giving her every bit as disdainful
had just given him.

'That rather depends. You see—'
the telephone in the kitchen started to
himself to Dee as he went to answer

'Yes, that's right,' she heard him sa
was calling. 'No, that's no problem. I
here anyway, so you can contact me h

tomatically sne walked towards the window, skirting past Hugo and the large pieces of Victorian furniture which dominated the room.

'What is it? What do you want to say to me?' Dee repeated tensely.

Hugo was frowning, looking away from her as though... Surely he...?

'Peter and I had a long chat after you'd gone last night...'

Dee could feel the violence of the heavy hammer-blows of her heart shaking her chest. Here it was: the blow she had always dreaded. Peter had spoken to Hugo, shared with him his doubts and fears about her father. Doubts and fears which he had never voiced to her, but which, like her, had obviously haunted him.

'He was telling me that your father...'

Dee closed her eyes, willing herself not to give in to the creeping remorseless tide of fear rising up through her body in an icy-cold wave.

'My father is *dead*, Hugo,' she cried out passionately. 'All he ever wanted to do was to help other people. That was *all* he ever wanted. He never...'

She stopped, unable to go on.

And then she took a deep breath, straightening her spine, forcing herself to look Hugo in the eye as she demanded huskily, 'What did Peter tell you?'

'He said that he was concerned about your plans to alter the focus of your father's charity. He told me that he was afraid that you were allowing yourself to be swayed by your emotion, and he said, as well, that he was afraid that you would try to pressure him into supporting you.'

Dee stared at him uncomprehendingly. Peter had talked to Hugo about her father's charity and *not* about his death. He had confided to him his fear of her desire to change things, his fear that...

The relief made her feel weakly light-headed. So much so that she actually started to laugh a little shakily.

'It's all very well for you to laugh, Dee,' Hugo chided her. 'It's obvious to me what you're trying to do. You want to steamroller Peter into supporting these changes you want to make, even if that means forcing him to act against his conscience.'

Dee fought to gather her thoughts. In the initial relief of discovering that Peter had not discussed her father's death with Hugo she had overlooked the gravity of what he was telling her. Now she was becoming sharply aware of it.

'Peter had no right to discuss the charity's business with you,' she reprimanded sharply. 'The charity is a private organisation run by the main committee of which *I* am the Chairperson. How that committee operates is the business of ourselves and ourselves alone—'

'Not quite,' Hugo interrupted her quietly, 'as I'm sure the Charity Commissioners would be the first to remind you...'

At this mention of the government body responsible for overseeing the proper management and control of charities Dee's eyes widened in indignation.

'We have no call to fear the Charity Commissioners,' she told Hugo firmly. 'Far from it.'

'I wasn't suggesting that you might,' Hugo responded coolly. 'However, this might be a good point at which to remind you that all your father's charities are overseen by that committee, and that whilst you *may* be the Chairperson of it, or them, you do *not* have the right to steamroller through whatever changes you wish to make.'

'To steamroller through…' Dee gasped in fresh indignation. 'How dare you? What exactly are you trying to suggest?' she demanded. 'My father's wishes are and always have been paramount to me when it comes to my role as—'

'Are they?' Hugo interrupted her. 'Peter doesn't think so.'

Dee sighed and took a deep breath, swinging round. 'My father wanted his own charity to benefit his fellow citizens. When he initially established it there was a need in the town to help the elderly, and that is exactly what we have done, but now… Things change…and I believe that our help is needed now far more by our young people.

'But none of this has any relevance to you, nor can it be of any interest to you,' she told Hugo firmly. 'I realise that to someone like you, who is used to dealing with the needs of people and situations a world away from what we are experiencing in Rye—people to whom the meagrest ration of food makes the difference between living and dying…'

She stopped, and then told him fiercely, 'The elderly in Rye are more than adequately provided for, but our teenagers...there's nothing for them to do, nothing to occupy or interest them. Ward says...'

'Ward?' Hugo interrupted her sharply.

'Yes, Ward Hunter,' Dee replied briefly. 'Ward has already put into operation—and very successfully— the kind of scheme *I* want to help establish in Rye.'

'Peter said that he felt that you were being influenced to break away from your father's ideas,' Hugo told her critically. 'And that's why—'

'Hugo, Peter means well, but he's old-fashioned. He can't see.' Dee paused and frowned. 'I really do need to talk with him to make him understand...'

'You mean to put pressure on him to go against his own beliefs,' Hugo told her caustically. 'Well, I'm afraid that just isn't going to be possible, Dee.'

'What? Why? What's happened?' Dee demanded, her heart immediately filled with fear for her father's old friend. Was there something about his health that Hugo was concealing from her?

'Why? Because this morning Peter asked *me* to act for him as his representative on the committee, and—'

'No...' Dee denied, grabbing hold of the edge of the table as she tried to control the shock that was making her body tremble. 'No, he *can't* possibly have done that.'

'If you wish to see the formal papers then I'm sure his solicitor will be happy to send you copies.'

'His solicitor?' Dee's voice faltered. 'But...'

'How does it make you feel, Dee, to realise that Peter felt concerned enough, distressed enough, to tell me that he wanted to sign a Power of Attorney in *my* favour so that I could deal with all his affairs because he was afraid that you might pressure him into doing something he didn't feel was right?'

Dee's face drained of blood.

It wasn't just the shock of hearing that Hugo would be taking Peter's place on her committee that was making her feel so sick with despair, it was also the heart-aching knowledge that Peter had felt that he couldn't trust her. Fiercely she blinked back the shocked, shamed tears she could feel burning the back of her eyes.

'Peter has given you Power of Attorney?' Dee asked weakly. She felt very much as though she would like to sit down, but her pride wouldn't allow her to betray that kind of weakness in front of Hugo of all people. She turned away from him and faced the window whilst she fought for self-control.

It seemed doubly ironic now, in view of what Hugo had just said, that she had actually entertained the thought of asking for his help in persuading Peter to give to her the very authority he had actually given to Hugo.

'Yes, he has,' Hugo confirmed. 'And you may be very sure, Dee,' he continued sternly, 'that I shall ensure his wishes are respected and that you do not ride roughshod over them. I dare say that you and this...this Ward Hunter believe that you have the power to bring the other members of the committee round to your way of thinking, but I can promise you—'

'The decisions of the committee have nothing to do with Ward,' Dee protested defensively. 'And in fact...'

'Exactly.' Hugo pounced triumphantly, overruling her. 'I'm pleased to see that you recognise that fact, even if that recognition is somewhat belated. From what Peter has been telling me it seems to me that you've been managing your father's charity very much as though it's your own personal bank account and that you—'

'That's not true,' Dee gasped angrily. 'Even if I wanted to do that—' She stopped and swallowed hard. 'What you're suggesting is... All I'm trying to do is to help those who need it most.'

'In your judgement,' Hugo pointed out.

'Hugo, Peter means well, but he's...'

'He's what? Not capable of making his own informed decisions any more?'

'No, of course not,' Dee protested.

'I'm glad. "No, of course not," indeed,' Hugo agreed. 'He tells me that the committee are due to meet soon to discuss their plans for the next twelve months. As his legal representative I shall, of course, attend the meeting on his behalf.'

Dee gulped.

'But you *can't*.'

'Why not?' Hugo challenged her coolly.

'Well, you might not be here. You must have business to attend to...'

'I shan't be going away—at least not in the foreseeable future. As I was just confirming to Peter's bank manager on the phone, I am free to work wherever I choose, and, since Peter needs to have someone close at hand to keep an eye on him right now, it makes sense for me to move in here with him.'

Dee felt cold all over, and tired, very tired. It appalled her that she, whom everyone considered to be so strong, could feel like this.

'You don't understand; *Peter* doesn't understand,' she started to protest.

'On the contrary, I think you'll find that I understand very well,' Hugo contradicted her flatly. 'Your father might have set up and funded his charity originally, Dee, but it is *not* your plaything. You do not have sole control over it; you and your boyfriend cannot simply—'

'Ward is *not* my boyfriend,' Dee was stung into replying, her face flushing with resentment at the way Hugo was talking to her.

'No? Well, whatever his relationship with you, Peter is very concerned about the influence he seems to have over you.'

'Peter is old-fashioned, set in his ways. He is wonderful, and I love him dearly, but he can be very stubborn, very blinkered.'

'He's only one member of a committee of seven people, Dee, and if he is the only one who does not share your point of view then I cannot understand why you should be concerned...'

Dee closed her eyes.

The fact of the matter was that Peter was *not* the only one likely to express doubts about what she wanted to do.

'Look, I've got an appointment in half an hour,' Hugo told her as he glanced at his watch.

As he spoke he was holding the door open for her, as though she were some candidate for a job and he had just finished interviewing her, Dee reflected angrily. She contemplated telling him that she was not going until she had spoken to Peter, and then acknowledged that there was little point in putting herself in an even more vulnerable position than she already was.

Head held high, she marched towards the open door.

'I shall see you on Monday,' Hugo told her cordially as she stalked past him. 'I understand that the committee meeting is set for eleven a.m.?'

'Yes, it is,' Dee agreed distantly, trying not to grind her teeth with vexation as he escorted her to the front door. How could Peter have done this to her? Put her in this position?

She could feel her fury and her frustration causing a tight ball of emotion deep inside her chest. As she passed him Hugo touched her briefly on her bare arm. Immediately Dee drew back from him, as though he had branded her.

'Dee, Peter is only acting out of concern—for you and for your father. He looks upon his role on the committee as an almost sacred trust, and he—'

'And you think that *I* don't?' Dee almost spat at him, her eyes burning with the intensity of what she was feeling as her gaze locked with his.

'Dee, your father set up this charity for a specific purpose, and I feel—'

'I don't care what you feel.' Dee cut across him furiously. 'You know nothing about my father, what he wanted, what he believed. You despised him be-

must have coaxed him to give him that Power of Attorney, Dee reflected darkly.

Perhaps it wasn't just the *university's* money Hugo was after for the United Nations aid programme. Dee smiled grimly to herself as she gave in to the temptation to give full rein to her ignoble thoughts.

. Peter was unmarried, with no family, and had a very healthy portfolio of investments—she should know; she was the one who had advised him on them. There had always been a tacit understanding between them that his money would be willed to her father's charity, but perhaps Hugo had other ideas.

Even though she knew she was allowing her anger to drive her thoughts and suspicions down extremely illogical routes, Dee refused to let go of them. Common sense told her that Hugo, even if he wasn't the scrupulously honest person she thought him to be, would not risk his reputation by doing something so potentially dangerous. Peter's money would be the merest drop in the ocean compared with the millions that Hugo would have under his control.

She looked at her desk. She was supposed to be seeing Ward this weekend, so that they could go over her proposals together for one final time.

To her consternation Dee felt the hot, painful tears of anger and disappointment filling her eyes.

Still prowling the room, she stopped her restless progression to study the large photograph of her father which she had had blown up and framed and which hung above the room's fireplace.

It was one of her favourite ones of him. In it he was just starting to smile, so that one could see the warmth in his eyes. He had been looking directly at her when the photograph had been taken—coincidentally, as it happened, by Peter—and whenever she felt really low Dee always drew strength from standing in front of it, right in his line of vision, so that she would feel again the warmth of his smile and his love.

This time, though, it wasn't totally effective. This time, knowing...remembering...how much her father had loved her could not totally ease the pain from her heart or the discord from her mind.

'You know nothing about my father...you despised him...' she had accused Hugo. It wasn't strictly true. What Hugo despised was the world he considered her father had represented: the world of money and prestige, of placing more importance on possessions than people. But her father hadn't been like that. He had been good with money, yes, and proud, very proud, but he had also been compassionate and caring, and it had hurt her more than she had ever been able to say to either of them that he and Hugo had not got on better together.

'But, Daddy, I love him,' she had told her father helplessly when he had questioned the amount of time she was spending with Hugo.

'You don't know what love is,' her father had objected. 'You're a girl still...a child...'

'That's not true. I know I love you,' Dee had defended herself firmly. 'And I'm not a child, nor even a girl now. I'm over eighteen...an adult...'

'An adult? You're a baby still,' her father had scoffed, and then added gruffly, '*My* baby...'

'Oh, Dad,' Dee whispered now, her eyes refilling

with tears. She had tried so hard to bring Hugo and her father closer. Too hard, perhaps. Certainly the harder she had tried, the more both of them had become entrenched in their suspicions of one another.

'How can he claim that he loves you?' her father had demanded once. 'What plans has he made for your future? The last time I spoke to him he told me that as soon as he'd finished his Ph.D. he was planning to take himself off to some desert or other.'

'Dad, he isn't so very different from you,' she coaxed her father. 'You both have very philanthropic natures and—'

'Maybe, but I would never have left your mother or you to go traipsing off all over the world,' her father interrupted her sharply.

Dee took a deep breath, knowing that the moment she had been putting off for so long could not be put off any longer.

'Dad, Hugo won't be leaving me,' she told her father quietly.

'Not leaving you? You mean he's changed his mind...seen sense?' her father demanded.

'No. Hugo hasn't changed his mind,' Dee answered him steadily. 'He still plans to go, but...' She paused, and then looked lovingly at her father. 'I'm going to go with him, Dad...'

'You're *what*?'

She had known he wouldn't be pleased, of course. Although no firm plans had been made she knew that he had hoped she would move back home after university, and until she had met Hugo she too had assumed that that was what she would eventually do.

Her father had never tried to hold her back, nor to impose his views on her. He had been the one to encourage her to leave home and go to university, but...but he wasn't really ready, deep down in his heart, to let her go completely yet.

'This is what Hugo wants. What do you want, Dee?'

I want you and Hugo to like each other. I want to be happy. I want Hugo, she could have said, but she knew that in his present frame of mind her father's heart was closed to the needs of her own. 'This is something I want to do for myself,' she told him quietly. 'I *have* to go, Dad. I love him!'

'Well, you're over-age, and I can't stop you,' he responded curtly.

Hugo loved her, too, she knew that, but he was fiercely, passionately determined to carry out the plans he had discussed with her. If she didn't go with him Dee knew he would go on his own. That didn't mean he would stop loving her—she knew he wouldn't—but it *would* mean that there would be a large slice of his life which she could not share.

Hugo was a crusader, a man who needed to live life on a grand scale, a young man full of the passionate intensity of his youth, and if Dee felt in her heart that her own inclinations lay closer to those of her father, if she felt that she could do just as much good working to help those in need at home as she could helping those who lived in such tragically difficult circumstances, if her dreams were smaller and gentler than those of the man she loved, then she felt that they were perhaps best kept to herself.

Hugo's family had already thrown enough cold water on his dream. Hugo needed her support and her love, and *she* needed to be with him.

In years to come the time they would spend together would be something they would remember, a memory that would help to bond them together, something to tell their children.

A small smile curled Dee's mouth.

Hugo might be all crusading male eagerness where his own life was concerned, but she knew instinctively that when it came to his children, to *their* children, he would want to protect them just as fiercely as her father did her.

In many ways they were so alike, so alike and so fiercely jealous of one another. Sometimes she felt like a bone they were both determined to possess.

In another few weeks she would sit her finals. Hugo had already completed his work, and their plan was that just as soon as they could they would leave together. Hugo had already approached one of the main aid agencies, and both of them had been provisionally accepted onto a scheme they were operating in Ethiopia.

Dee had suggested that before they left they should both spend time with their respective families, but Hugo was impatient to leave just as soon as possible.

Although officially they still had separate homes, Dee now spent most of her time at Hugo's and she had her own key. Her father might logically guess that she and Hugo were lovers, but Dee was sensitive enough to know that he would not want to have such suspicions confirmed. He came from a generation when a couple's sexual life was something strictly private, and really only acceptable inside the respectable confines of a marriage. Dee knew that it was different for her and Hugo, of course. The thought of how it would feel not to have the freedom to reach out into the night and touch Hugo's naked body, not to know the special pleasure of knowing that body so well that it was almost as though, in some way, it had become hers, was simply unbearable, and not just because of the sexual frustration she would suffer. She loved Hugo so much that she wanted to be close to him in every way there was.

Emotionally, mentally, physically and of course sexually, they had no secrets from one another, no prohibited areas. Dee loved lying in bed and watching as Hugo padded around the bedroom, his naked body as splendidly magnificent as that of a male cheetah in his prime. Everything about him sang with energy and health, from the silky, sleek gleam of his skin to the thick, shiny glossiness of his hair.

It still amused—and amazed—her to see the way he could respond physically to her just because she was looking at him.

'*You're* the one who's caused it,' he would tease her as his busy perambulations about the flat became halted by the demanding urgency of his arousal. 'So now it's up to you to do something about it.'

'Such as what?' she would ask, mock innocently, all the while her fingers delicately caressing him.

'Mmm...well, that will do for a start,' he would murmur to her as he covered her mouth with his own, his weight pushing her back against the pillows.

They had been together for over two years, but the intensity of their physical desire for one another still had the power to awe and excite Dee. She only had to run her fingers teasingly along the length of Hugo's erection, or just merely circle its head and caress it playfully, for him to immediately be so responsive to her that her own body flowered into delirious response. Sometimes, in the middle of a serious discussion, she would reach across and touch him temptingly, laughing as he tried to hold on to the thread of his argument, her eyes betraying the wonderment and awe she still felt that he should love and want her so much.

They had their quarrels, of course. Both of them were strong-willed and passionate, both of them felt things very deeply, and both of them were very vocal in stating those beliefs, but the only real issue of contention which existed between them was that of Dee's father. She had introduced them to one another with loving pride—and anxiety—and soon discovered that she had been right to be anxious.

The evening had ended with her father and Hugo arguing passionately about the morality of the government in power; her father had been pro-government and Hugo anti. Torn between both of them, she had tried to placate her father, knowing how it would hurt his pride to have to acknowledge the strength of Hugo's arguments. But then later, when they had returned to Hugo's flat, Hugo had claimed that she had supported her father against him, and not just that but, even worse, she had denied her own beliefs as well.

'You know as well as I do that I was right,' Hugo had told her fiercely, for once refusing to respond to the loving little kisses she'd been pressing placatingly along his jaw. 'You've agreed with me that—'

'Dad's old-fashioned and set in his ways,' she had told Hugo. 'I didn't want to hurt him...'

'But you don't mind hurting me,' Hugo had challenged her grimly.

She had sighed and wrapped her arms lovingly around his neck.

'Does it matter which of you won the argument?'

'Yes,' Hugo had told her simply, before pointing out more acerbically, 'If it didn't you wouldn't have found it necessary to side with your father, would you?'

'I meant, does it matter to you?' Dee had countered placatingly. 'It isn't easy for Dad, you know Hugo, having to accept you into my life.'

'It isn't easy for me having to accept him into ours,' Hugo had retorted. 'One day you're going to have to choose which of us your loyalty really lies with,' he had warned her.

But Dee had crossed her fingers behind her back, telling herself that, given time, the pair of them would become better friends. And perhaps they might have done if Hugo had been more willing to give ground to her father and listen to his advice, even if he didn't act on it, or if her father had been able to accept that Hugo needed to be allowed to feel that her father respected his viewpoint even if he couldn't agree with it.

As it was, with neither of them prepared to give

do it it's because…because I love and want you, but when it's him, it's because… He makes my skin crawl, Hugo…there's something about him that I just don't like. I don't trust him…'

'Tell your father, not me,' Hugo had counselled her.

'He wouldn't listen,' Dee had admitted uncomfortably.

Hugo's eyebrows had risen, his mouth curling cynically as he'd commented, 'No…but according to you your father is a man of reason and compassion, a man who is *always* willing to listen to the views of others. Others, but not, it seems, to me or to you…'

'Hugo, that isn't fair,' Dee had protested. 'We're talking about two different things. My father—'

'Your father is jealous because you love me,' Hugo had told her flatly, 'and until you accept that fact I'm afraid you and I are never going to see eye to eye over him.'

'Now you're doing what you always complain my father does,' Dee had told him angrily. 'Now you're trying to put emotional pressure on me. Hugo, I love him…he's my *father* and I want so much for the two of you to get on well together…'

'Have you told *him* that?' Hugo had asked her wryly.

It was an argument that was destined to run and run, and of course it had.

'Have you told him yet?' Hugo asked Dee that evening.

'Yes,' she acknowledged tiredly.

'And…' Hugo prodded. 'Or can I guess?'

'He wasn't very happy,' Dee admitted.

'So, tell me something I don't already know,' Hugo drawled. 'I suppose he claimed that you would be wasting your degree and the government's money, that you'd be exposing yourself to almost certain death, that I was being a selfish so-and-so and that I should stay at home and get myself a proper job…'

His comments were so acutely right that Dee felt her eyes prick with vulnerable tears.

'Hugo, he's my father; he loves me. He's just trying—'

'To come between us?' Hugo suggested bitterly.

'He just wants to protect me,' Dee protested. 'When you…we…have children, you'll feel the same.'

'Maybe I shall, but I certainly won't put emotional pressure on them or try to control their lives for them,' Hugo told her tersely.

'Julian Cox arrived whilst I was there. It sounds as though he's trying to persuade Dad to put him on the Foundation committee.'

'So?' Hugo questioned.

'I don't trust him, Hugo. There's something about him.'

'He's not my type, I agree,' Hugo replied, 'but then I've never been into making money, so…'

'Maybe not, but that's because *you've* never needed to be,' Dee responded, with an unusual touch of asperity. 'You get an allowance, Hugo, as well as your grant. One day you'll inherit family money—even though you claim your parents aren't wealthy. My

father has had to make his own way in life. He's
proud of what he's achieved and so am I, and I hate
it when you go all aristocratic and contemptuous
about him. There's nothing wrong about being good
at making money.'

'Isn't there?' Hugo asked her quietly. ' My great-
great-grandfather made his from coal, from sending
people deep down into the earth to dig for black gold
for him. There's a plaque outside the colliery that he
owned. It commemorates the deaths of twenty-nine
men who were killed making my great-great-
grandfather a millionaire. He gave their widows a
guinea each. It's all there in his accounts. Like your
father, *he* had a good head for money. I used to dream
about them sometimes, those men, and how it must
have felt to die like that.'

'Hugo, don't,' Dee pleaded, white-faced. Hugo
rarely talked about his family history, but Dee knew
how he felt about it.

As she turned towards him Hugo cupped her face
in his hand as he begged her hoarsely, 'Don't ever
leave me, Dee. Don't let your father come between
us. I love you more than you know. You've enriched
my life, made my life better in so many ways. Without you...'

'Without me you'd still go to Ethiopia,' she told
him quietly.

His eyes darkened.

'Yes,' he agreed simply, before adding harshly, 'I
have to, Dee. I can't... I have to. But I shan't be going
without you,' he added softly. 'Shall I?'

He was kissing her by then, and so there was no

vocal reply that Dee could give other than a soft, blissful sigh as she moved closer to his body.

Later, their bodies closely entwined, Hugo leaned over her propping his head up on his elbow as he told her quietly, 'Dee, there's something I have to say to you.'

'Mmm...?' she encouraged him languorously.

It wasn't unusual for him to tease her with this kind of pronouncement, which was usually followed by a declaration of his love or an announcement that some part of her body was filling him with unquenchable desire, and so, smiling back at him, she waited happily.

'This aid work—it isn't just something I want to just do to fill in a year,' Hugo told her abruptly.

Dee sat up in bed. She knew already how strongly Hugo felt about what he wanted to do, but this was the first time he had mentioned it being more than a short-term vocation.

'I was talking to someone the other day, and they were saying how desperately they need people to take on not just work in the field but fundraising as well.'

'But you can't do both,' Dee objected practically.

'Not at the same time,' Hugo agreed. 'But there's a desperate need for people to increase everyone's awareness of how vitally important good aid programmes are, to act as ambassadors for them. Charlotte was saying that I'd be ideal for that kind of role, especially once I'd got some practical hands-on experience in the field.'

'Charlotte?' Dee queried uncertainly.

'Mmm...Charlotte Foster. You don't know her.

She graduated a year ahead of me and she's been working for a children's charity. She's just come back to this country and I bumped into her the other day in town.'

Dee listened in silence.

'It will perhaps mean that I shall have to spend longer in the field than we'd planned.'

'You mean it might mean that *we* are going to have to spend longer in the field than *we* had planned,' Dee corrected him gently. She saw instantly that she had said exactly the right thing.

'I *knew* you'd understand,' Hugo exulted as he hugged her tightly. 'It will mean having to put off having a family for rather longer than we agreed.'

He shook his head and groaned.

'Charlotte was telling me that they go into the most unbelievable details before taking people on their permanent staff. There have been so many scandals involving people misusing charity money that now they check and double-check to make sure there's absolutely no chance that anyone they employ carries even the merest whiff of scandal. Charlotte told me that they've recently asked one of their executives to leave because his stepfather turned out to have been under suspicion of being involved in some kind of financial fraud. But then, of course, you can understand why they have to be so careful.'

'Mmm…' Dee agreed.

'You're wonderful. Do you know that?' Hugo told her happily. 'The ideal woman for me…the ideal wife!'

* * *

The next few days were busy ones for Hugo. His decision to make his commitment to working for an aid charity a permanent rather than a temporary one meant that, with Charlotte's encouragement, he was toing and froing from Lexminster to London, seeing people and being interviewed.

'There's so much we still need to learn,' he told Dee excitedly one afternoon, after he had returned from a briefing session with the agency Charlotte had recommended him to.

'We're finding that the people themselves actually teach us how we can best help them. Charlotte says—'

It was less than a month until Dee sat her finals. She had been studying when Hugo had rushed in, and, despite Hugo's insistence that Charlotte was simply a friend, to Dee it was quite obvious that the other woman was in love with him. Her patience snapped.

'I don't care *what* Charlotte says,' she told him sharply. 'There are other things in life, you know, Hugo, like the fact that I've got my finals in four weeks' time.'

'You'll pass them,' Hugo assured her cheerfully. 'Look, Charlotte's invited us out for a celebratory dinner tonight.'

'A celebratory dinner?' Dee queried.

'Mmm… She's pretty sure that I'm going to be offered a permanent post with the agency. Come on, you can shower first.'

'Hugo, I can't go out…not tonight,' Dee protested, indicating the books in front of her. 'I've *got* to study. Look, you go,' she told him in a gentler voice. She hated having to spoil his pleasure, but she still had to break the news to her father that they would be gone longer than they had originally planned, and that Hugo intended to make a permanent career in the aid field—which meant that they would be travelling the world for most of their married lives, Dee suspected. There was no way she could study with Hugo prowling the flat in his present electrified, excited state. She would be able to work far better if she was on her own.

'Well, if you're sure you don't mind,' Hugo said.

'Mmm…I love you,' he whispered to her half an hour later, just before he left. Smiling at him, Dee returned his kiss.

'You can show me how much later,' she teased him.

Oddly, once he had gone she found it almost impossible to settle back into her work. On impulse she went over to the telephone and dialled her father's number.

He answered almost straight away, and Dee could tell from the way he said her name that he had been hoping that she might be someone else. That alone was enough to make her frown. Her father was *never* too busy to speak to her when she phoned—in fact he was always complaining that she didn't ring often enough— and besides, some sixth sense, some daughterly awareness, made her instantly pick up that something was wrong.

'Dad—' she began urgently, but he was already cutting her off, telling her curtly,

'Dee, I have to go. I'm expecting another call…'

'Dad,' she protested, but it was too late. He had already hung up.

Dee waited ten minutes and then rang again, but the line was engaged. It was still engaged when she tried a second time and then a third.

It was now nearly ten o'clock, but, late though it was, Dee knew that she just had to see her father.

Scribbling Hugo a note, she hurried out to her car.

CHAPTER EIGHT

THE phone rang abruptly on Dee's desk, breaking into her thoughts of the past. Automatically she reached for the receiver. Her caller was Ward Hunter, and after Dee had asked after Anna's health, Ward began, 'Look, I've been thinking. It might be a little unorthodox, but if you'd like me to come along and talk with your committee, explain to them how we've gone about things and—'

'Ward, I'd love you to, but I'm afraid it won't do any good. There's a problem.'

Briefly Dee outlined to him what had happened.

'You say this man has somehow persuaded Peter to give him Power of Attorney? Who is he, Dee? Is he related to Peter or—'

'He's not related to him but they are old friends,' Dee interrupted him. 'In fact, I...I actually know him myself,' she added reluctantly.

'Oh. I was just thinking that it might be worthwhile making some enquiries to see if he had put any kind of pressure on Peter to...'

'No. No, I don't think there's any question of that. He's very high up in one of the main aid agencies, Ward, and from what I know of him...' She stopped, unwilling to go on. No one in her present life knew anything about Hugo, and that was the way she

127

wanted things to stay. After all, what was the *point* in them knowing?

'Mmm…what I can't understand is why this Hugo, whatever his name is, has decided to oppose your plans, when anyone with any sense can see how beneficial they would be.'

'Hugo thinks he's on a moral crusade,' Dee told him wryly.

'Well, don't give up yet,' Ward encouraged her. 'Surely there's still a chance that you can persuade the rest of the committee…?'

'A very remote chance,' Dee agreed. 'A *very* remote chance.'

Five minutes after she had said goodbye to Ward the telephone rang again. This time it was Beth who was telephoning her.

'Dee, how are you?' she asked cheerfully. 'I saw you in Lexminster today. Why didn't you call and see me?'

Beth and her husband-to-be were living just outside the town in a pretty eighteenth-century farmhouse they had recently bought. Alex was the university's youngest chair. He lectured in Modern History whilst Beth still owned and ran the pretty glassware shop in Rye-on-Averton with her partner, Kelly, which she rented from Dee.

'I would have loved to but I didn't have time,' Dee fibbed.

'No, I understand. Anna mentioned that you're busy with your plans to open a workshop along the lines of Ward's. Well, if you want someone to teach your teenagers all there is to know about making glass, Alex's aunt is due over this summer, and, believe me, *no one* knows more about it than she does.'

Dutifully Dee laughed. She had met Alex's aunt, and she knew that she was very much the matriarch of the Czech side of Alex's family.

'Look, I was wondering if you might be free for supper on Saturday night. I know it's short notice, but Alex is having to entertain someone—something to do with setting up a new scholarship.'

'If this someone is a he and you're—' Dee began firmly, but Beth anticipated her and laughed.

'He is a he, but I promise you I'm not trying to matchmake. Please, Dee.' Beth was beseeching her.

Unwillingly Dee gave in. The last thing she really felt like doing was being sociable.

'Seven-thirty for eight, then,' Beth informed her, ringing off smartly before Dee could change her mind.

It was dark by the time Dee eventually let herself into the house that had been her father's. It had been dark too the night she had driven home in such anxiety, slipping her key into the lock and hurrying into the hallway, calling her father's name.

He hadn't answered her, and it had been a shock to go into the kitchen and find him sitting there, immobile and silent.

Equally shocking had been the sight of a bottle of whisky on the table beside him and an empty glass. Her father rarely drank, and when he did it was normally a glass or maybe two of good wine.

'Dad...Daddy,' she pleaded anxiously, her heart

plummeting as he turned his head to look at her and
she saw the despair in his eyes.

'Daddy, what is it? What's wrong?' she asked him,
running over to him and dropping to her knee in front
of him. They had never been physically demonstrative
with one another, but almost instinctively Dee took
hold of his hands in both of hers. They were frighteningly icy cold.

'What is it...are you ill...? Dad, please...' she
begged him.

'Ill...?' His voice cracked harshly over the word,
sharp with bitterness and contempt. 'I *wish*... *Blind*,
that's what I've been Dee, corrupted by my own pride
and my vanity, my belief that I knew...' He stopped,
and Dee realised that the tremors shaking her own
body were coming from his. It shocked her immeasurably to see him like this, her father, who had always
been so strong, so proud...

'Dad, please—*please* tell me what's wrong.'

'You shouldn't have come here. What about your
finals...? Where's Hugo...?'

'He...he had to go out.'

'So he isn't here with you?'

She could see the relief in his eyes.

'At least I'm spared *that*, although it can only be
a matter of time and then everyone will know.'

'Know what?' Dee demanded.

'That I've been taken in by a liar and a cheat, that
I've given my trust to a thief and that he's... Gordon
Simpson rang me last week,' he told her abruptly.

Gordon Simpson was the manager of the local
branch of their bank, and a fellow committee member

with her father on the local branches of two national charities.

'He's been going through the charity accounts with the accountant, and certain anomalies have come to light.'

'Anomalies…what, accounts mistakes, you mean?' Dee asked him, perplexed. She knew how meticulous her father was about such matters, and how annoyed with himself he would be at having made a mistake, but surely not to this extent.

'Accounting mistakes? Well, that's one way of putting it.' He laughed bitingly. 'Creative accounting is how the gutter press prefer to refer to it—or so I'm told.'

'Creative accounting.' Dee's blood ran cold. 'You mean *fraud*?' she asked him in disbelief. 'But that's *impossible*. *You* would never—'

'No,' he agreed immediately. '*I* would never…but Julian Cox… He deceived me, Dee, took me in completely. He's cheated the charity out of a good few thousand pounds already, and all under my protective aegis. Oh, Gordon told me that no one would hold me to blame…he said he'd been as convinced of the man's honesty as I was…but that doesn't matter. *I* am still the one who was responsible for allowing him to become involved. I am still the one who vouched for him.

'Of course, I've repaid the missing money immediately, and Gordon and Jeremy, the accountant, have given me their assurance that the matter won't go any further.

'I tackled Cox immediately, and do you know what

he had the gall to say to me? He told me that…he tried to blackmail me, Dee. Me! He threatened to go to the press and tell them that I'd supported him, encouraged him, unless I agreed to let him get away with it.

'Gordon and Jeremy said there was no point in pursuing him legally, and that to do so would bring the matter into the public arena and damage people's faith in the charity. They said that since I'd offered to refund the money the best thing to do was to simply keep the whole thing quiet.'

'Oh, Dad,' Dee whispered helplessly. She knew how strongly her father felt about matters of law and morality, and how much it must be hurting him to have to tell her. It wasn't just his pride that had been damaged, she knew, it was his whole sense of self, his whole belief about the importance of honesty.

Dee tried her best to comfort and reassure him, but she felt helplessly out of her depth. He was, after all, her father, and a man, and he was also of a generation that believed that it was a father's and a man's duty to shield and protect his womenfolk from anything that might cause them pain.

He had, Dee recognised, always sheltered her from the unpleasant things in life, and it frightened her to see him so vulnerable, so alarmingly unlike himself.

She spent the night at home with him. When she rang Hugo to tell him what she was doing there was no reply to her call, and, illogically, some of the anger and resentment she felt against Julian Cox she transferred to Hugo, for failing to know of her need and thus failing to meet it.

In the morning her father's air of restless anxiety made her feel equally on edge. He had someone he needed to see, he told her evasively when he came back downstairs for the breakfast she had prepared, but which neither of them ate, but when she asked him who he refused to answer her.

Since she had last seen him he had lost weight, and his face looked gaunt. Dee's heart ached for him. How could Julian Cox do this to her father?

'You haven't done anything wrong,' she told him fiercely. 'It's Julian Cox and not you.'

'Nothing wrong legally, maybe, but I still let him make a fool of me. I trusted him and, what is worse, I trusted him with other people's money. Who's going to believe that I didn't know, that I wasn't a party to what he was planning to do?'

'But Dad, *you* don't need the money.'

'*I* know that, Dee, and so do you, but how many other people are going to question my honesty? How many are going to believe there's no smoke without a fire?

'You'd better get back to Lexminster,' he told her wearily. 'You've got your finals in four weeks.'

'I've got plenty of time to study.' Dee fibbed. 'I want to stay here with you, Dad. I'll come with you to this meeting...I—'

'No.'

The sharpness of his denial shocked her. She had rarely seen him angry before, never mind so frighteningly close to losing control.

'Dad...'

'Go back to Lexminster, Dee,' he reiterated.

And so, stupidly, she did. And that was a mistake; an error of judgement; a failure to understand that she would never, ever forgive herself for.

If Julian Cox was responsible for her father's death, then she was certainly a party to that responsibility. If she had refused to go back to Lexminster, if she had stayed with him...

But she didn't... She drove back to Lexminster, desperate to see Hugo and tell him what had happened, running in fear to him, like a child denied the comfort of one strong man's protection and so running to another.

But when she reached the house Hugo wasn't there.

He had left her a note, saying that he had been called to London unexpectedly to attend another interview and that he didn't know when he would be back.

Dee wept in a mixture of anger and misery. She wanted him *there* with *her*, not pursuing some selfish, idealistic dream. She *needed* him there with her, and surely for once *her* needs came first. Was this how it was going to be for the rest of their lives? Was Hugo *always* going to be missing when she needed him? Were other people *always* going to be more important to him than her? She was too wrought up to think or reason logically; it didn't make any difference that Hugo had no idea what was happening—it was enough that he just wasn't there.

Anxiously Dee rang her father at home. There was no reply. She tried his office, and gritted her teeth as she listened to the vague voice of the middle-aged spinster he employed as his secretary more out of pity for her than because he actually needed her help. She lived with her widowed mother and three cats, and was bullied unmercifully—both by her mother and the moggies.

'Your father—oh, dear, Andrea, I'm sorry; I have no idea... He isn't here—'

'He said he had an appointment with someone,' Dee told her, cutting across her. 'Is there anything in his diary?'

'Oh, let me look... There's a dental appointment— but, no, that's the fifteenth of next month. Just let me find the right page. Oh, yes...here we are. And it isn't the fifteenth today at all, is it? It's the sixteenth... No...he *was* to have seen that nice Mr Cox for lunch today...'

She paused as Dee made a fierce sound of disgust deep in her throat. What was loyal Miss Prudehow going to say when she learned just how un-nice 'nice Mr Cox' actually was? When she learned just what he had done to Dee's father—her employer?

Five minutes later, having extracted from her the information that she had no idea where Dee's father was, Dee replaced the receiver and redialled the number of her father's home. Still no reply. Where was he...?

It was later in the day when she knew. Early in the evening, to be exact.

The young policeman who came to give her the news looked white-faced and nervous when Dee opened the door to him. After he had asked to come in, and followed her inside the house, Dee noticed how he was unable to meet her eyes, and somehow, even before he said her father's name, she knew.

'My father?' she demanded tautly. 'Something's happened to my father...'

There had been an accident, the young policeman told her. Her father had been fishing. Quite what had happened, no one was sure. But somehow or other he had ended up in the river and got into difficulties. Somehow or other he had drowned.

Dee wanted badly to be sick. She also wanted badly to scream and cry, to deny what she was being told, but she was her father's daughter, and she could see that to give in to her own emotions would upset the poor young policeman, who looked very badly as though *he* wanted to be sick as well.

Dee had to go back with him to Rye. There were formalities to be attended to but not, thankfully, by her. She wanted to see her father, but Ralph Livesey, his friend and doctor, refused to allow her to do so.

'It isn't necessary, Dee,' he told her firmly. 'And it isn't what he would have wanted.'

'I don't understand,' she whispered, over and over again and throughout it all. 'How *could* he have drowned? He was such a good swimmer and...'

As she looked at Ralph she saw the look in his eyes, and instantly a sickening possibility hit her like a blow in the solar plexus.

'It *wasn't* an accident, was it?' she whispered sickly to him. 'It wasn't an accident.'

Her voice started to rise as shock and hysteria gripped her. 'It wasn't an accident. It was Julian Cox...he did it. He killed him...'

'Dee,' she heard Ralph Livesey saying sharply, before turning to the policeman who was still there and telling him, 'I'm afraid she's in shock. I'll take her home with me and give her something to help her calm down.'

Once he had bundled her into his car Ralph Livesey was grimly relentless with her.

'Whatever *you* might think, Dee, so far as the rest of the world is concerned your father died in a tragic accident. I don't want to cause you any more pain. I can understand how upset you are, but for your father's sake you *have* to be strong. To make wild accusations won't bring him back, and could actually do him a lot of harm.'

'Harm? What do you mean?' Dee demanded.

'There's already some disquiet in town about...certain aspects of your father's professional relationship with Julian Cox.'

'Julian tried to deceive Daddy. He lied to him,' Dee defended her father immediately.

'I'm quite sure you're right, but unfortunately your father isn't here to defend himself, and Julian Cox is. To suggest that your father might have taken his own life will only exacerbate and fuel exactly the kind of gossip he would most want to avoid.'

'You mean that Julian is going to get away with *murdering* him?' Dee protested sickly. 'But...'

'I understand how you feel, Dee, but Cox did *not* murder your father. No one did. My guess is that he slipped off the bank whilst he was fishing. We've had a lot of rain recently, and the ground is treacherous. He lost his balance, fell into the river, probably knocking himself unconscious as he did so, and whilst he was unconscious, very tragically, he drowned.'

Dee looked at him with huge pain-filled eyes.

'I *can't* believe it was an accident,' she whimpered to him. 'Dad was a strong swimmer and—'

'It was an accident,' Ralph Livesey told her firmly. 'That is my judgement as a doctor, and I believe it is the one your father would have wished for.'

It was almost a week before Dee was able to leave Rye and return to Lexminster. There were formalities to attend to—formalities relating to her father's business affairs which, as Dee might have expected, had been left in meticulous order. Meticulous order, maybe, but someone would have to take over the business, someone would have to stand in her father's shoes. Dry-eyed, Dee had calmly made a brief list of those who might be able to do so, and then equally calmly she had put a cross through them all. There was only *one* person who could be trusted to carry on the work her father had been so dedicated to— only one person who could ensure that his memory was forever enshrined in the hearts and minds of the townspeople with all the respect and love to which he was entitled—and that one person was her.

Once she had made her decision she made it known to her father's solicitors, now hers, and all those people he had worked most closely with.

'But, Dee, whilst I applaud your desire to do this, it really isn't practical,' her father's solicitor told her. 'For one thing you've still got your finals ahead of you, and for another…'

Dee closed her eyes, and on opening them looked at him and through him.

'I'm not going back to university,' she told him distantly. How could she? How *could* she leave Rye? How could she leave her father's name and reputation unprotected and vulnerable to the likes of Julian Cox? She had made the mistake of leaving her father unprotected once, and look what had happened. She wasn't going to do it again. It never occurred to her that she might be in shock, or that her emotions might be warped and twisted by the sheer intensity of what had happened.

She had made her decision.

Hugo would have to be told, of course, but she doubted that he would care very much. If he cared he would be here with her, wouldn't he? If he cared he would have saved her father, wouldn't he? But he hadn't done. Had he?

Two days after her father's death, and the day before his funeral, she had a telephone call from Hugo.

'Dee, what on earth…? I've been ringing the house for the last two days. What are you doing in Rye?'

'I had to come home,' she told him bleakly.

'Look, I'm not going to be back for another few days. Whilst I was having my interview they told me that someone had dropped out of one of their training programmes, and they asked me if I'd like to take his place. It will speed things up by about six weeks, since they only run these induction programmes every two months, but of course it's meant that I've had to put everything else on hold.

'They do it here in London, in-house, and they're putting me up with one of the guys who works for them. Dee, it's fascinating, but it makes me feel so inadequate. There's just so much to learn and know.

Some of these people are still farming using methods that date back to biblical times, and…'

Still numb from the trauma of her father's death, Dee was only distantly aware of Hugo's selfish absorption in himself, and his total lack of awareness of her own need, her own pain and anger—emotions which fused together to make her feel that she had to protect her father, not just from Hugo's lack of love for him but also from his patent lack of awareness that anything was wrong with her. And so, deliberately, she said nothing—after all, why should she? Hugo quite obviously didn't care. Somewhere deep inside she knew that somehow this discovery was going to hurt her, and very badly, but right now all that mattered was her father—not her, and most certainly not Hugo and his precious interview!

'Hugo, I've got to go,' she interrupted him unemotionally.

'Dee…? Dee…?' she heard him demanding in astonishment as she replaced the receiver.

The phone rang again almost immediately, but she didn't answer it. She couldn't.

Tomorrow her father was to be buried, but Hugo was more interested in the farming methods of people he didn't even know than in her father's death and her own pain. Her father had been right to question Hugo's love for her. And even if he did love her as much as he had always claimed to…as much as she loved him…there was no future for them together now, Dee recognised. How could there be? Her place was here, in Rye. It had to be. She owed it to her father.

Dee closed her eyes. Right now she couldn't think

about where Hugo's life and future lay. Right now all
she could think about was that Julian Cox had destroyed her father...taken his life...and that it was
down to her to ensure that nothing else was taken
from him, that his reputation remained intact—and
not just intact but revered and honoured.

Hugo tried to talk her out of her decision, of course,
but she had remained obdurate. Her refusal to answer
the phone had caused him to come straight back to
Lexminster, but by then Dee's resolve had hardened.
All that she allowed herself to remember of their relationship was that Hugo had never loved her father
and how important his ambition was to him—far
more important than her.

'But, Dee, we love each other,' he pleaded with
her, white-faced and patently unable to take in what
she was telling him.

'No,' she announced, averting her face from his. 'I
don't love you any more, Hugo,' she lied. 'My father
was right; it would never have worked between us.'

She couldn't tell him why she had to stay. He
wouldn't have understood.

A part of her ached for him to tell her that there
was no way he was going to accept her decision, that
there was no way he was going to let anything come
between them even if it meant giving up all his own
plans, but she knew, of course, that he would never
do so. His plans meant too much to him—as much
as her father meant to her.

'Dee, let someone else take over your father's business affairs,' Hugo pleaded with her.

'I can't,' Dee told him sharply.

'Why…what's so damned important about making a few more hundred thousand pounds?' he challenged her angrily.

Dee shook her head. She could have told him that it wasn't the money she needed to protect, it was her father's reputation—but how could she tell him that her father had taken his own life? That he had been on the brink of being branded a cheat and perhaps even worse?

It wasn't so very long ago that Hugo had been telling her just how important it was that his *own* reputation was above reproach. How would she feel at the thought of potentially being contaminated by the slur on her father's reputation via *her*? And if she was not there to protect him there was no saying what damage Julian Cox might do to the memory and the name of her father. He hadn't gone for good, Dee knew that instinctively. He would be back, and who knew what malicious rumours he might choose to spread when he did return?

'Dee…I don't understand,' Hugo was saying helplessly. 'Is there someone else? I know your father…'

'Don't talk to me about my father.' Dee responded fiercely. 'It's over, Hugo. It's over. If you can't accept that then I'm sorry… I have to go now,' she told him stiffly, standing up.

'You have to go now… Just like that… Just as though we're two mere acquaintances instead of—' he began savagely. 'You and I are lovers, Dee…we planned to marry, to raise a family. You wanted to have my child, my *children*,' he reminded her grimly, 'and now you're acting—'

'Acting!'

Dee's body quivered. Hugo mustn't suspect the truth, mustn't ever know just what it was costing her to do this, to send him away, but she had to do it. She had to do it both for her father's sake and his own.

'I've changed my mind,' she told him.

He reached for her then, and she read the purpose in his eyes even before his mouth crushed down on hers. She stood motionless in his embrace until he lifted his head, and then she told him in a dry, whispery voice, 'If you do, now, Hugo, it will be rape...'

He let her go immediately of course. She had known he would. He stormed out of the house, his face white with bitterness and anger.

She didn't cry then, and she didn't cry the following day either, when she buried her father.

She remained at the graveside for over an hour after the other mourners had gone, and when she eventually turned to leave she saw Hugo, watching her from several yards away.

He made to come over to her, but she shook her head and walked quickly in the opposite direction, balling her hands into fists in the pockets of her coat, her body stiff with a mixture of fear and rejection. She didn't dare let him see how vulnerable she felt, or how much she longed for him, how much she wanted him...how much, already, she ached for him and missed him.

It simply couldn't be. How could it? Her place wasn't with him any longer.

At Dr Livesey's insistence, after the funeral she went to stay with her father's aunt in Northumberland for several weeks. When she returned there were several notes in her post from Hugo, begging her to get in touch with him. She burned them all. And then, six weeks after her father's death, she woke up one morning like someone coming out of an anaesthetic or a long paralysis, the pain of her returning un-numbed emotions so intense that the agony of them almost made her scream.

Hugo!

Hugo! What had she *done*? Not only had she lost her father, she had sent away the man she loved, the only man she would ever love.

Hugo!

Hugo!

She dialled the number of his Lexminster flat and then, when there was no reply, she drove over to Lexminster to find him.

The shock of discovering that his flat was empty, and then of learning from a neighbour that Hugo had left for Somalia the previous day, made her reel with sick shock.

He had gone.

She had lost him.

It was over.

Now there was no going back.

Hugo!

Hugo!

CHAPTER NINE

'WARD, I'm worried about Dee.'

Ward Hunter replaced the financial section of the paper he had been reading and looked across the breakfast table at his wife.

They had been married less than a year, and he marvelled that he could have managed to live so long without her. Just the sight of her pretty face on the pillow in the morning had the power to lift his heart to a degree that left him shaken with the depth of their love.

The fact that she was carrying their child only increased his awe that life should have thought him worthy of such munificence.

'You mustn't worry,' he chided her tenderly, adding a little bit more dryly, 'Especially about Dee. She's more than capable of running her own life, and running it extremely well.'

Anna gave a small sigh. Much as she loved her husband, there were some things, some signs, that only another woman could fully appreciate and understand.

Dee was very self-sufficient, very strong and independent, yes, but Anna was an extremely intuitive woman and she was concerned about her friend.

'What exactly did she say to you about there being

a problem with her plans to establish a unit like yours?' Anna asked Ward thoughtfully.

'Not much. Just that,' Ward responded unhelpfully. 'But that won't be worrying her. Not Dee. She thrives on having something to get her teeth into.'

'Mmm...'

Ward had a point, but Anna was still not totally reassured. She made a mental note to telephone Dee, or, even better, to call round and see her.

Grimly Dee opened her front door and let herself into her house. She had just spent the morning and the best part of the afternoon going round trying to discreetly canvass some support for her plans from the other committee members, but so far their reaction had not been reassuring.

Only the bank manager shared her view on how important it was to make the changes she wanted to make.

As she walked into the kitchen she dropped her files on the table. One of them contained her carefully worked out and detailed proposals for what she wanted to do and the other, which she had taken to discuss with her solicitor, was the original deed which had been drawn up when her father had first instituted the charity.

His depressing but expected advice had been that there was no loophole via which she could push through her proposals without the support of Peter Macauley—in other words, Hugo.

'I sympathise with what you want to do, Dee,' he

had said, 'but without the agreement of Peter's representative on the committee, it just isn't possible.'

'I've got my own funds,' Dee had reminded him. 'If I use them...'

'I can't possibly advise you to do that,' he had counselled her sharply. 'You're still only a young woman. You have your own future to think of. You already make a very substantial personal donation to the charity and—'

He had stopped, shaking his head, and Dee had known that he spoke the truth. It was her responsibility to manage the funds in the foundation her father had set up, and to this end, with Dee's agreement, he had placed most of his personal wealth in that foundation.

Whilst Dee had certainly been left adequately financially provided for by her father, she had not, by any means, been left the vast fortune other people thought. The fact that she was now a reasonably wealthy woman owed more to her adroit financial management of her own assets than to her inherited wealth, and Dee was pleased that it should be that way. But, like him, she preferred to donate most of the money she made to the local charity he had established, rather than amassing it for herself. But no one knew better than she did herself just what her ambitious scheme was likely to cost. There was no way she could fund it by herself—not in the immediate future.

How *could* Peter have done this to her?

She filled the kettle and went to stand by the sink, looking out into the garden as she waited for it to boil. Pointless, though, to blame poor Peter; he was only following the dictates of his conscience.

The doorbell rang. Dee was tempted to ignore it. The last thing she felt like right now was having to be sociable, but, as she hesitated, it rang again.

Squaring her shoulders, she went to answer its summons.

As she opened the front door, initially a beam of bright sunlight semi-dazzled her, so that for a moment she actually thought she must be seeing things. She blinked quickly once, and then once again, but no, she was *not* seeing things. He, Hugo, was actually standing there.

'Hugo,' she protested dizzily as he stepped towards her, but it was too late to protest or to deny him admittance because he was already standing in her hallway.

'What is it? What do you want?' she demanded sharply as she closed the door.

'I had to see you,' he responded. 'We need to talk.'

The sombreness of his voice and his expression immediately aroused Dee's anxiety.

'What is it?' she repeated as she led the way to the kitchen. 'Is it Peter? Is he worse? Is he...?'

As she opened the kitchen door and Hugo followed her inside the telephone rang in her study.

Excusing herself to Hugo, she went to answer it.

'Dee, it's me, Anna,' she heard her friend announcing as she picked up the receiver. 'I thought I'd just ring for a chat. How *are* you? Ward told me about the problems you're having with the committee—'

'Er, Anna, can I ring you back later?' Dee interrupted her quickly. 'It's just that…I'm rather busy at the moment.'

Dee didn't want to offend Anna, but she knew there was no way she could talk to her with Hugo in the house.

'Yes. Of course. I understand,' Anna agreed immediately, but Dee could sense that she was a little surprised.

Replacing the receiver, Dee hurried back to the kitchen. As she opened the door she could see Hugo standing by the table holding her file that related to the plans she had hoped to put to the committee. He was quite blatantly reading the file, and angrily Dee demanded, 'What are you doing? Those are private papers.'

'Are *these* the proposals you were planning to put to the committee?' Hugo asked her brusquely, ignoring her angry demand.

Dee glared at him.

'Yes, as a matter of fact they are. Not that it's any business of yours.'

Abruptly she stopped, remembering too late just exactly what business it actually was of his, but it was too late now to recall her childish taunt.

A little to her surprise, though, instead of picking her up on it Hugo merely continued to frown and returned his attention to her open file.

'Your proposals call for a very radical change in direction for the charity,' Hugo told her.

Through her open study door Dee could hear her fax machine clattering.

Impatiently she looked from Hugo towards the

study. The fax could be important. In some of the markets in which she had dealings a delay of only minutes in a deal could mean a financial loss of many thousands of pounds.

Turning her back on Hugo, she hurried back to her study, ripping the printed message out of the fax machine and quickly running her glance over it.

Body found in sea off Singapore identified as that of Julian Cox. Singapore authorities are investigating possibility of murder as Cox known to be a heavy gambler with large outstanding debts. Any further instructions?

The message had been sent via the agency Dee had used to try to trace the whereabouts of Julian Cox, and, although she had always known that wherever he had gone he would sooner or later return to his dishonest, cheating ways, she had not expected to receive news like this.

She closed her eyes, and then opened them again and reread the message. How ironic. How quixotic of fate—if it *was* Julian Cox—that he should be found drowned...just like her father.

Dee started to shiver, a low, agonised moan whispering dryly past her from her taut throat.

'Dee? Dee, what is it? What's wrong?'

Dee was vaguely conscious of Hugo coming into her office and taking the fax from her, but the message, coming on top of her recent mental reliving of the events leading up to her father's death, was having a dangerously traumatic effect on her. She knew that

Hugo was there, she knew he had taken the fax from her and she knew too that he had read it, but even though she knew all these things somehow they were not completely real to her. What *was* real…*all* that was real…was that Julian Cox was dead: he had now gone beyond her justice, and beyond any earthly court of law's jurisdiction. The judge he now had to face…

'Cox is dead,' she heard Hugo saying. 'I didn't realise he meant so much to you. You never seemed to care very much for him.'

'*Care…*' Dee could feel something splintering sharply inside her, lacerating her so painfully, emotionally *and* mentally, that the agony of what she was experiencing made her want to scream out loud.

'Oh, yes, I *care*… I care that he cheated and deceived my father. I care that he nearly destroyed everything my father had worked to achieve. I care that he threatened him with humiliation and I care that my father trusted him and believed in him whilst he was cheating him. I care that because of him my father died…I care that he caused my father to take his own life. I care that because of him I lost *the* man—'

As Dee put her hands up to her face she discovered to her own bemusement that it was wet and that she was crying, that her hands were trembling, her body shaking violently. She was, Dee recognised distantly, dangerously close to losing control.

'Dee, what are you saying?' she could hear Hugo demanding curtly. 'Your father and Cox were partners, close friends…'

'Julian Cox was no friend to my father,' Dee denied chokily. 'He threatened him with blackmail…

Oh, God…why did I let it happen? Why didn't I stay with him? If I had, Dad would still be alive today and I…'

She stopped. She would what? She would have been married to Hugo…the mother of his children…?

'I should have stayed, but I didn't…I was so selfish…I wanted to get back to you. I never dreamed that Dad would take his own life, that Julian would drive him to take his own life. He must have been so afraid, so alone. I let him down so badly.'

'Dee, your father *drowned*,' Hugo told her gently. 'It was an *accident*.'

'No… My father drowned, yes, but it *wasn't* an accident. How could it have been? He was an excellent swimmer, and why would he have gone fishing anyway? He told me that he had a meeting.'

She was shivering violently, her body icy cold but her face burning hot.

'Dee, you've had a bad shock,' she could hear Hugo telling her softly. 'Why don't you come and sit down in the kitchen and I'll make us both a hot drink? Come on. You're cold; you're shivering,' he told her when Dee started to shake her head in violent denial of what he was saying.

'I don't *want* a drink. I don't want *anything*… I just want you to go.'

It was over. At long last it was over. At long last there was no need for her to pursue Julian Cox any more. Fate had stepped in and taken over, but oddly Dee couldn't feel relieved. She couldn't in fact feel anything, only an aching, agonising awareness of how senseless, how wasteful her father's death had been.

For the first time since her father's death Dee was able to admit to herself that, alongside her pain and her anger against Julian Cox, there was also a sharp thorn of anger inside her against her father—anger that he could have done what he had done without thinking how much it would hurt her, how much she would miss him…how much she loved him. She had always known how important other people's respect had been to him, how much he'd valued it—but surely not more than he'd valued her?

But he had left her, turned his back on her and her love for him, her need for him, and ended his own life. And she had been left alone to face the consequences of what he had done. Her eyes filled with fresh tears, a searing animal moan of pain escaping her lips. She was shivering, freezing cold, but suddenly she was aware of a sense of blissful warmth and comfort as Hugo crossed the small space between them and took hold of her.

'Dee, you're not well. Let me call your doctor.'

'No,' Dee protested immediately. Her doctor was still Dr Livesey, and she didn't want to see him. He had been the one who had insisted her father's death was an accident.

'Well, at least let me help you upstairs.'

Dee tried to resist. There wasn't anything wrong with her, not really. It was just the shock, the relief of knowing that it was over, that Julian Cox wasn't going to be able to taunt or torment her any longer.

There had been so many times over the years when she had longed to be able to share her feelings with someone else, when she had longed to be able to tell them what had happened, but she had never dared allow herself to give in to that temptation. It was as though in some horrible Faustian way she had struck a deal with the devil—the devil in this case being Julian Cox himself. As though by keeping her silence she was ensuring that he kept his, that he didn't attempt to besmirch her father's memory. Although logically, of course, Dee knew that he couldn't have done so without risk of exposing himself. There had been periods when he had actually lived away from Rye, no doubt practising his deceitful, dishonest ways somewhere else, but he had always returned.

Now, though, he couldn't harm anyone any more. Not her father, not Beth, not anyone. It was over.

She frowned in bewilderment. She was in her bedroom, but she had no recollection of having walked upstairs. Hugo was closing her bedroom door.

'Dee, is there someone I could ring—a friend you'd like to have here with you?' Hugo was asking her.

Immediately Dee shook her head, cringing mentally at the very thought of having to explain to anyone.

'I just want to be on my own,' she told Hugo shakily. 'I just want to be left alone.'

She felt most peculiar, oddly light-headed and so cold still. She wanted to crawl beneath the covers of her bed and lie there. She didn't want to see or speak with *anyone*.

She was only a few feet away from the bed, but for some reason as she tried to walk towards it her feet felt almost too heavy for her to lift. The bed wavered and dipped as she tried to focus on it, the floor tilting. She gave a sharp cry of protest and another softer one of shock as suddenly Hugo was next to her, supporting her, holding her.

Holding her!

Dee closed her eyes, longing flooding through her—a longing that was so intense, she could feel it in an actual physical inner pain. With her defences down, shot to pieces, the mantra she had taught herself, that Hugo belonged to her past and love was something she had learned to live without, no longer had the power to work, even if she could have remembered it.

Suddenly she was a girl again, longing for the security of her lover's arms, wanting him so much, aching for him so intensely.

'Hugo.'

As she whispered his name she wrapped her arms tightly around him, closing her eyes, ecstatically breathing in the scent of him.

'Hugo.'

She turned her head, desperately seeking his mouth with her own.

She heard him say something, her name, a plea…a sound. It didn't matter.

His hands were cupping her face, his lips, his mouth responding to the hungry passion of her own.

Once, a lifetime ago, they had kissed like this as hungrily and needfully as this, unable to take the time to draw breath properly, their hearts thudding in rapid unison, the passion between them building to such a pitch that it was almost too much to be endured.

Once, a lifetime ago, she had already experienced

this need to lose herself completely in him, to be absorbed totally into him, to become somehow a part of him, so that the two of them were one indivisible whole.

Frantically Dee clung to him. She had lost him once, just as she had lost her father. Her father was lost to her for ever, but Hugo was here, alive, warm, *real*.

Passion—the kind of passion that allowed nothing to stand in its way, that swept down like an avalanche, swamped like a tidal wave, burned a path like a forest fire—gripped her, filling her, leaving no room for anything else.

She might as well have been blind, deaf and dumb for all the attention she paid to the logical warnings of her brain.

She heard Hugo groaning, and her senses recognised the sound, receiving it, registering it and interpreting it. Her hands slid feverishly down his back, past his waist, spreading against the hard masculine shape of his buttocks, pressing him into her own body just as when, long ago, that soft little groan had been a signal and an invitation for her to touch him in just that way, a sensual message from him that he wanted her to touch him, that he wanted her to show that she was responding to his desire for her and that she welcomed his arousal. So now Dee responded to it as such, trembling a little in the ferocity of her own passion as she felt the unmistakable hardening of his body.

'Dee...'

His voice was low, raw with longing, liquid with need, roughened by a soft burr of warning.

'Yes. Yes, I know,' she whispered back to him between the hungry kisses they were still exchanging.

'Undress me, Hugo,' she begged him. 'Quickly, I can't wait.'

As though to prove her point, she started to tug at her own top, moaning a little in frustration when he didn't immediately come to her aid. Hugo had never been the kind of lover who had allowed their lovemaking to drift into a stale routine, a familiarity that meant that he no longer had to court her, and automatically she abandoned her attempts to remove her own clothing and turned instead to the much more exciting task of removing his, tugging frantically at the buttons on his shirt, muttering little absorbed sounds of protest as her fingers refused to work fast enough to satisfy her urgency.

'Hugo, help me,' she demanded feverishly. 'I want to see you, *touch* you...*taste* you... Hugo...'

She gave a small gasp of satisfaction as the button she was tussling with finally came free exposing the upper half of his chest. Impatiently she tugged at another, and then another, so totally absorbed in her task that she wasn't fully aware of the sudden tension that gripped Hugo's body and the way he drew in his breath in a swift, sharp gasp. His skin was slightly darker now than she remembered it—his time spent in the field was responsible for that, no doubt—and the muscles beneath his skin were somehow more solid, heavier, stronger, just as the silky sprinkling of dark hair she remembered as being quite light was

now thicker, different, somehow far more dangerously masculine and exciting.

Since she was not in the habit of studying men's
bodies, and since there had been no intimate relation-
ships in her life since Hugo had left it, she had no
way of comparing him with any other man, but Dee
knew instinctively that his body, at once both so familiar and yet at the same time so pulse-racingly different, was a kind of body that very few men of his
age possessed. Wonderingly she touched the soft hair
that shadowed his skin, and then very deliberately followed the line it made down the length of his torso.

'Dee.'

The hoarse explosive sound of protest he made
shocked her into stillness. Questioningly she looked
up into his eyes.

'Dee!' he said again, and then as he looked back
into her eyes he stopped and groaned, closing his own
eyes and then opening them again to tell her rawly,
'Come here… If you're going to torment me like that
then I'm going to do a little tormenting of my own.'

His fingers were much defter on the fastenings of
her clothes than hers had been with his shirt. It took
him only seconds to remove her silk blouse and the
bra she had been wearing under it. His hands were
on the waistband of her trousers when she leaned forward and delicately started to nibble at his throat,
tender little biting kisses of a type he had always
loved.

As her trousers slithered to the floor his hands
swept up, cupping her breasts, moulding and caressing them, the pads of his thumbs rubbing urgently

over her already stiff nipples. Dee moaned his name and pressed her hot face into the curve of his shoulder, the urge to rake her fingers down the length of his back so strong that she had to fight not to give in to it.

The shock of the news of Julian's death coming so hard on the heels of the even greater shock of seeing Hugo again had totally destroyed the protective walls she had built around her feelings, leaving her achingly aware of how much she loved him, how intensely she longed for him. They were so powerfully strong that she couldn't find the words to express them. All she could do was to try to show him, smothering the hard warmth of his chest with her kisses, stroking the smooth flesh of his back, making small keening noises in her throat as he reciprocated and touched her.

Her body remembered every touch, every stroke, every fingerprint of his hands against her; remembered them and responded to them, her nails digging into his skin in frantic pleasure as he lowered his head and started to kiss the soft flesh of her breasts. Dee trembled from head to foot, unable to understand how she had been able to bear to give up such savagely sweet pleasure, how she had been able to live without it and without him.

The ferocity of her need made her moan in soft frustration as she tried to press her body closer to his and felt the thick fabric of his jeans rubbing against the softness of her own bare skin.

'Hugo... Hugo...' she protested.

'What is it? What's wrong?' she heard Hugo asking her thickly.

'This is wrong,' Dee responded passionately, her fingers plucking at his jeans. 'I want to feel you. *You*, Hugo. I want to see you, touch you.' Her voice started to rise a little as her feelings rioted out of her control. She could see Hugo's reaction to her need in the way his eyes darkened, a dark red tide of male arousal colouring the taut flesh of his face.

'You want me…you want this…?' she heard him demanding thickly as he reached for his belt and started to unfasten it.

Once, long ago, as a young girl, she might have looked modestly away. But she was a woman now, not a girl, and Hugo was a man. *Her* man.

Her mouth was soft and red, swollen by the passion of their shared kisses, her eyes dark and filled with open longing as she followed the movement of his hands. Deep down inside her own body she knew how much she wanted him. She held her breath, her body tensing as he removed the rest of his clothes. The very maleness of him almost took her breath away. She had seen him like this before, of course, but for some reason the impact of him on her now was a thousandfold more dangerous than she could ever remember it being before.

Unable to stop the long, low sound of female need that escaped from her throat, she put her fingertips to her lips.

'Don't do that,' Hugo warned her hoarsely, and then he was reaching for her hand, carrying her trembling fingers to his own mouth which he brushed softly against the sensitive pads of her fingertips. Dee felt her whole body turn wantonly liquid, and then begin to burn with shocking heat.

Very slowly and deliberately Hugo began to lick her captive fingertips, and then even more slowly to suck them. He was looking straight into her eyes, and even though she knew just what he could see in them, and how impossible it was for her to hide her reaction from him, she wanted him so much that it physically hurt—agonisingly so, so much so that she had to close her eyes against the hot burn of her pain.

'Dee. Dee… don't…don't cry…please don't cry,' she heard Hugo begging her hoarsely, dropping her hand to cup her face and reinforce the intensity of his words with suffocatingly tender kisses that inflamed her even more rather than soothed her. Unable to stop herself, she reached out and touched him, her fingers trembling a little at first as they enclosed him. His flesh felt smooth and hot, the shape and texture of him so instantly and vividly remembered that automatically she was already caressing him, stroking him firmly and possessively, knowing just how he liked her to touch him and where. This was *her* territory, *her* love, *her* man.

'Dee…'

She heard the warning in his voice but she was oblivious to it, totally lost in the fiercely sensual pleasure of caressing him.

'Dee…' Hugo warned her thickly again, when she failed to heed his warning. But Dee didn't want to listen. She could feel Hugo's hands on her body, hot and heavy, and their movement dictated the fierce pulse Dee could feel thudding against her stroking touch.

She was wearing a pair of tiny silky briefs, the merest wisp of fabric. She could feel Hugo tugging impatiently at them, but even without feeling them slither to the floor she would have known the moment she was free of them from the way Hugo suddenly sucked in his breath and the tension she could feel in his body.

He had once told her, both of them giddy, dizzy with satisfied passion, how much he loved the way the silky triangle of dark hair between her thighs so delicately hid the secret of her sex, and she had responded in kind, her eyes soft with love as she had compared the soft silkiness of her own body hair to the much thicker and more vigorous curls that surrounded his own sex. Now that contrast between them, which as a girl she had simply taken for granted, had an almost primitive effect on her senses. *Now* it made her feel intensely aware of his maleness, his potency, so much so that her body physically shook with the force of her awareness of him and of it.

'You're just the same. You haven't changed,' she heard Hugo whispering rawly to her. 'And I've never forgotten—*never*.'

Unable to stop herself, Dee felt the first of her pent-up emotional tears splash down on the hand he had lifted to touch her.

'Dee, what *is* it...? What's wrong...? Oh, Dee. Dee, don't, please, my darling. Please don't cry,' she heard Hugo begging her as he wrapped her in his arms and picked her up.

'I'm not crying. I'm not crying,' Dee denied. 'I just want you inside me so much that it hurts, Hugo. Please don't make me wait any longer...please.'

'Dee. I can't...I haven't got—'

'You can,' Dee protested fiercely, reaching out to touch him. He was so strong, so ready for her. How could he say otherwise when she could feel how much he wanted her?

She pulled away from him and walked unsteadily towards her bed, climbing onto it and holding out her arms to him.

It seemed to take a lifetime for him to reach her, and another for him to join her, to take her in his arms and kiss her, slowly, almost reluctantly at first, and then with a hunger that was almost elemental, almost savage. But something within her responded to his urgency, something within her wanted it, she recognised, as his hand parted her thighs and his fingers found the moist readiness of her.

'No, it's not that I want. It's you,' Dee told him thickly. 'I want you, Hugo, you...'

She cried out as he entered her. It had been so long, and she wanted him so much. Her body was so exquisitely sensitive to him that each thrust of him within it filled her with an almost unbearable surge of pleasure.

She had known him like this so many, many times before, and yet this was different, Dee acknowledged. This went beyond the satisfaction of a mere physical need, beyond the mutual pleasure of reaching a sexual pinnacle.

The urge to let herself reach the climax of her pleasure was almost unbearably strong, but something made her delay it; something made her urge him to thrust even deeper inside her, as deep inside her as it was possible for him to reach, because that way...

Unable to control her longing any more, Dee cried out in abandonment. Deep within her body she could feel the hot pulse of Hugo's release, so deep within her body that she could feel her womb physically contract. A strange feeling filled her, an unfamiliar sense of giving in to fate, to a power stronger than her own.

'Hugo.'

Lovingly she traced the shape of his mouth with her fingertip.

'I never really stopped loving you, you know. I had to send you away, though, because of Dad.' Fresh tears filled her eyes.

'Dee, you can't really believe that your father took his own life,' Hugo protested as he kissed her and brushed them away. 'I know that he and I didn't see eye to eye, but there is no way, in my opinion, that he would ever have done something like that, no matter what kind of pressure he came under.'

'Is that what you really think?' Dee asked him uncertainly.

'Yes, I do,' Hugo confirmed. 'Your father was a strong man Dee, a good man. He loved you far too much to do something that would hurt you.'

'Julian Cox's deceit humbled him, Hugo. Humiliated him. He had trusted him, believed in him. For him to have discovered that Julian had been using his patronage to steal money... Dad paid it all back, of course, but...'

Dee yawned deeply.

'I feel so tired,' she complained. 'I still can't totally believe that Julian Cox is dead, or that...'

She yawned again, more deeply this time.

'Go to sleep,' Hugo told her gently, leaning over to kiss her mouth.

Obediently Dee closed her eyes.

Hugo waited until her breathing told him that she was fast asleep before easing himself out of bed. Peter was due to see the heart specialist whom the doctor had called in this evening, and Hugo had promised he would be there with him.

There hadn't been time for him to say to Dee all the things he had wanted to say. Her disclosures about her father had filled him with pain and pity. They had always been close, and he could understand how it must have hurt her to think of her father taking his own life, but despite what she had told him Hugo felt sure that his death had been a genuine accident.

It was strange how things worked out. He had come here today, driven by an impulse, a *need* so strong that no amount of logic had been able to prevent him from responding to it. Even though every bit of common sense he possessed had told him that he was a fool to even think of approaching Dee and telling her how he felt, asking her if there was any way she was prepared to give the love they had once shared a second chance, he had still felt compelled to do so.

What had actually happened between them was nothing short of miraculous. Dee still loved him. He was older now, and wiser too, and he could recognise that, much as he had loved Dee as a young man, there *had* been a certain selfishness in him, a certain single-mindedness which had driven him to pursue his own goals, his own dreams, and to expect Dee to make them hers.

Things were different now. It hadn't taken him very long to discover that without Dee his ambitions, his dreams had become curiously unfulfilling. There had been the satisfaction of knowing that what he was doing was for the benefit of others, but there had also been the loneliness of living his life on his own. Not that he hadn't had plenty of discreet and sometimes not so discreet offers of female companionship and love, but no other woman could possibly measure up to Dee.

He had told himself that, in choosing to put her love for her father above her love for him, Dee had been the one who was the loser, but when he had received the news that she was married and expecting a child he had known just which of them was the one to suffer the most.

If he hadn't been given that mistaken bit of gossip would he have acted differently? he mused as he dressed and quietly went downstairs, letting himself out of the house.

He would let Dee sleep off the trauma of the day and then, once Peter had seen the specialist, he would ring her, invite her out for dinner, take her somewhere discreet and romantic where he could...

Humming to himself, he unlocked his car.

Oh, yes, if he hadn't thought she was married and out of reach, he suspected that he would have come back sooner. Much sooner. And if he had...

Immediately his imagination conjured up an image of two children: a boy with his mother's eyes and a girl.

Oh, yes, he still loved her...had never stopped loving her...and right now—before he reversed his car out of her drive he glanced up towards Dee's bedroom window—right now the temptation to go back into the house and stay with her was so strong that... But he owed it to Peter to be with him.

Peter.

He grimaced ruefully to himself. Peter had rather misled him with his anxiety over Dee's proposals, and he could see that he was going to have to have a talk with him.

Dee!

He didn't dare start thinking about her, Hugo recognised. Not now. Not whilst he was driving.

CHAPTER TEN

DEE woke up abruptly from the dream she had been having. In it she had been walking with her father along the river. He had been holding her hand, just as he had done when she had been a little girl, smiling at her as he'd paused and pointed a shoal of minnows out to her as they swam busily in the reeds. The water had been so clear she had been able to see the bottom of the river.

Further out from the bank, though, the water had been much deeper, and suddenly she had felt afraid, drawing back, gripping her father's hand tighter, but he had laughed at her, telling her that there was nothing to be afraid of and that he loved her.

There were tears on her face, Dee recognised, but they were tears of love. As she sat up she noticed a piece of paper lying on the empty pillow beside her.

Uncertainly she picked it up, her heart thumping heavily as she recognised Hugo's handwriting.

'I love you', he had written.

I love you.

Dee closed her eyes. Hugo loved her and Hugo had told her that he didn't believe her father had taken his own life. She slid out of bed and padded over to her bedroom window. It was almost dusk, and Hugo's car had gone from her drive. She had no idea where he

had gone, or why, but Dee knew instinctively that he
would come back.

'I love you', he had written, and coming from
Hugo those words meant exactly that. He loved her.

Her body ached in odd, unfamiliar and yet somehow very familiar little ways and places. She could
still smell Hugo's scent on her skin, and if she closed
her eyes she could almost feel the touch of him beneath her fingertips. She had no idea what lay ahead
of them.

Hugo could, he had told her during their argument
at Peter's, live virtually wherever he chose. His role
within the aid programme was no longer one that re-
quired him to work out in the field. *Her* work demanded that she live here in Rye-on-Averton, but if
the committee refused to sanction the changes she
wanted to make to the charity she wasn't sure that
she wanted to remain involved in it. Her father's charity could be carried on without her direct involve-
ment, and without her fearing any damage to her father's name. She had no responsibility, no duty to
keep her in Rye now. She could move, live wherever
she wished, go with Hugo wherever *he* wished. *If* that
was what he wished.

'I love you', he had written. Not, I want you, I need
you...with me always...as my partner, my wife, the
mother of my children.

Children. Dee touched her stomach. Did Hugo
know, as she had known, had he felt as she had felt,
that fierce pulse, that fusion, that heartbeat of time
which had created a new life...their child? Or was it
just a woman's thing, a woman's special secret

knowledge, that awareness that her own body was no longer exclusively her own?

Hugo's child conceived within her. Her father would have loved to have had grandchildren.

Her father.

Dee closed her eyes and then opened them again. Was Hugo right, or had he simply been trying to comfort her?

She went to the bathroom and showered quickly. There was something she had to do. Somewhere she had to go.

'Well, now that Mr Stewart has been able to put Peter's mind at rest, he certainly won't need to be so dependent on you,' Jane told Hugo briskly.

They were in the kitchen of Peter's house. The specialist had left, having examined Peter thoroughly and then declared that he was extraordinarily fit for a man of his age and likely to live at least another ten years. But the doctor had lingered on after he had gone.

'He feels very vulnerable and alone,' Hugo told her.

'Mmm... Well, you mustn't allow him to become too dependent on you, you know. After all, you have a right to a life of your own,' she added, with a coy look, before continuing, 'Speaking of which, I was wondering if you'd like to have dinner with me one evening.'

Hugo smiled gently at her.

'It's very kind of you, but I'm afraid I can't...'

Couldn't and certainly didn't want to. The only woman he wanted to be with was Dee—the only woman he had ever wanted to be with, the only woman he would ever want to be with.

It had been his pride that had prevented him from pleading with her to change her mind all those years ago when she had told him it was over between them, and if he had known then just *why* she had said it... But she had taken good care that he shouldn't know.

It was later than he had hoped before he could leave. Peter had wanted to talk over the specialist's comments, and Hugo hadn't had the heart to cut him short or show any impatience.

'You're going out? But it's late,' Peter protested when Hugo explained.

There was no reply to the brief phone call he made before he left Peter's, and he assumed that Dee must still be asleep. But when he pulled into the driveway of her house he saw that her car was missing and he started to frown.

He hadn't said, of course, that he would come back that evening, but somehow he had assumed that... That what? That she would be there waiting for him with open arms...?

He grimaced ruefully as he felt his body's reaction to his thoughts.

He could stay here in his car and wait for her to return, but suddenly Hugo thought he knew where she might have gone. It was an instinct, a gut feeling, with nothing logical or practical to back it up, but nevertheless he set his car in motion, driving through the town.

A dozen or more teenagers were sitting on the benches in the town square, obviously at a loose end.

Dee's report had surprised him, and made him feel rather ashamed of the judgements he had made.

As he drove through the town he could see his destination ahead of him—or rather its spire.

The first time she had brought him to Rye-on-Averton, Dee had pointed out the pretty parish church to him. Her parents had been married there, she had told him, and she'd hoped she would be. Many generations of her family were buried in its graveyard, including her father.

As he drove into the close that led to the church he saw Dee's parked car. Sometimes it paid to listen to one's instincts.

The graveyard was quiet and shadowy, but it was a pleasantly peaceful place rather than a threatening one, Dee acknowledged. She had never been here at night before, although she had visited it many, many times during the day, especially in the early days after her father's death, with the rawness of her own heartache. Now the scars were softer. She touched her father's headstone and traced the words carved there.

'*Was* I wrong, Dad?' she asked him huskily. 'Was it really an accident after all? It hurt me so much to think that you'd deliberately left me,' she told him conversationally. 'To feel that your pride and other people's respect for you were more important to you than my love. I hated Julian Cox for what he'd done, and sometimes I almost felt as though I hated you as well.

'Hugo says you would never have taken your own life. Never have hurt me by doing such a thing. You

were always so quick to criticise him, and he you, but
I knew it was just because both of you loved me. I
hated having to choose between you, but how could
I go with Hugo, leaving you to face the fear which
had driven you to your death on your own? I had to
stay...I had to protect your reputation from any harm
that Julian Cox might do to it.'

'Dee...'

She froze, and then swung round as she recognised
Hugo's voice.

'Hugo...what are you doing here? How did you
know...?'

'I just knew,' he told her gently as he came towards
her, stopping just a few feet away from her.

'I had to come here,' she told him simply. 'I had
to...to talk to Dad...to ask him...to—'

'Dee, why *didn't* you tell me what you feared?'
Hugo interrupted her softly. 'Surely you could have
trusted me.'

'I could have trusted you, yes,' Dee agreed quietly,
'but I couldn't burden you with my...my doubts,
Hugo. You'd already told me how important it was
that you had an unblemished reputation. For me to
tell you that I thought my father might have taken his
own life, that he could have become embroiled in a
sordid fraud case... I couldn't do it to you. I...I
couldn't expose my father to *you*, and I couldn't expose *your* reputation to...

'And besides...' Dee looked away from him '...I
felt that I wasn't important enough to you...that your
plans, your ideals mattered more, and I was afraid...I
was afraid of committing myself completely to you,

Hugo, because I feared that you wouldn't commit yourself completely to me.'

'So you told me you didn't love me any more. Was it true, Dee?'

Dee shook her head.

'No. Never,' she told him in a raw whisper. 'I wanted you to come back. I wanted to tell you that I'd changed my mind. But you never did...'

'No?' Hugo gave her a wry look. 'I managed to last six months in the field without you and then I had to come back, but when I did I heard that you'd got married, that you and your husband were expecting a child.'

'It wasn't true,' Dee told him, shaking her head. 'My cousin married, but...'

'Perhaps I should have asked more questions...probed more deeply. But I was so shocked, so bitterly hurt that... I think I hated you then, Dee,' Hugo told her gruffly. 'There's never been anyone else for me...no one ever came close to making me feel the way you did...do...'

'No, it's been the same for me. I...I wanted a family...a child...children...so desperately at times, Hugo, that I almost contemplated... But...' She paused. 'In the end I just couldn't. I couldn't bear my child to have any father but you.'

She looked down at the gravestone.

'Do you *really* think it was an accident?'

'Yes, I do. A tragic, senseless, wasteful accident—but still an accident, Dee.'

'An accident...' Dee touched the stone tenderly

and then, lifting her fingertips to her mouth, she kissed them softly and then touched them to the stone.

'Goodbye, Papa,' she said softly, using the pet name she had had for her father as a little girl. 'May you rest in peace.

'I think maybe you're right,' she told Hugo, her eyes brilliant with unshed tears as she added huskily, 'I hope that you are right.'

'I am right,' Hugo promised her, and he held out his hands to her and commanded, 'Come here. I've missed you so much, Dee, wanted you so much—so much more than I've ever allowed myself to know. But today, holding you...touching you... I couldn't endure to lose you again. I don't know how I've endured these years without you.'

Dee stood up and let him take her hands in his and draw her towards him. The warmth of his hands wrapped around her own filled her with the most intense sense of peace, of release, and somehow, as she went to him, Dee suddenly knew that he was right, that her father hadn't taken his own life.

With that knowledge came a lifting of her heart, her spirits, that made her feel almost light-headed, buoyant, filled with such a sense of joy and love that the intensity of her emotions seemed to make the air around her sing. Like a weight slipping from her shoulders and from her heart she could feel all the animosity she'd had, all the anger, all the bitterness she had felt towards Julian Cox leaving her like ice melting in the warmth of the sun. There was no room in her heart any more for such dark and painful feelings, because now it was overflowing with the joy of rediscovering the love she shared with Hugo.

'Let's go home,' Hugo suggested simply.

'Home!'

Dee gave him a whimsical smile as she let him guide her back to where their cars were parked.

'And where exactly might that be?'

They had reached the edge of the graveyard, and as he led her through it and onto the road outside Hugo turned her towards him and told her as he bent his head to kiss her, 'Home for me is where *you* are, Dee. *Wherever* you are.'

He followed her back to her house, parking his car behind hers, taking the key from her trembling fingers to unlock the door and then kicking it shut behind him before taking her in his arms and kissing her.

'How did you know where I was?' she asked him when he released her.

'I don't know...I just did. I had planned to take you out somewhere special for dinner. It's a bit late for that now.'

'Mmm...' Dee agreed, and then added teasingly, 'It looks like you'll have to think of some other way to satisfy my...hunger...'

'Oh...I thought I'd already done that,' Hugo responded just as teasingly, adding suggestively, 'But of course, if that wasn't enough...'

'Hugo!' Dee exclaimed. 'What about Peter? He—'

'Peter's going to be fine. That was why I went back.' Quickly he explained to her about the specialist's visit.

'Which reminds me—these proposals of yours...'

Dee tensed. Surely they weren't going to quarrel so soon?

'I'm not prepared to change my mind about them, Hugo,' she warned him quickly. 'Not even for you. I know how Peter and the others feel, but I truly believe that there is a genuine need—'

'I agree.'

Dee stared at him. 'You do?'

'Mmm...and from what I've read of your proposals I have to admit that I can't really understand just *why* Peter is so opposed to them.'

Dee sighed. 'Neither can I—not really. But he is getting old, and he's very set in his ways.'

'I'll try and talk to him,' Hugo promised her. 'Unfortunately, morally, if nothing else, whilst I'm acting as his Power of Attorney I have to vote as he would wish to have done.'

'I understand that,' Dee assured him gravely.

'I have to *vote* as he would have done, but that doesn't mean that I can't make my own assessment of the situation and try to persuade him accordingly,' he told her.

'I thought you'd have enough to do lobbying the university authorities without lobbying Peter on my behalf,' Dee told him ruefully. 'Is it really fair, though, Hugo, to try to persuade the university to use funds that are meant to be used for the benefit of scholars' charitable work to help finance aid programmes, no matter how deserving they might be?'

Hugo gave her an astonished look.

'Is *that* what you think I'd do? You're wrong. The

reason I want to speak with the university authorities is to try to persuade them to introduce a vocational course for students to educate them about the way we work and the way they can help us. We need young, keen, innovative brains to come up with solutions to the problems we're constantly facing—but right now what I need most of all is you.'

'Me...?' Dee looked at him mock innocently.

'Mmm... You,' Hugo repeated.

This time they made love slowly and tenderly, luxuriating in every touch, every kiss, sharing their joy at their mutual discovery of each remembered pleasure and adding new ones to them.

'You're even more beautiful now as a woman than you were as a girl,' Hugo told Dee as he stroked his fingertips along the soft warm curves of her body.

'And *you* are even more dangerously sexy,' Dee told him, glaring mock angrily at him as he threw back his head and laughed. 'You don't believe me? Ask Dr Jane Harper,' she challenged him.

'Who's Dr Jane Harper?' Hugo demanded huskily as he bent his head to tease the erect nipple he had just been stroking.

Dee closed her eyes and gave a soft moan of liquid pleasure.

'I felt so *jealous* of her,' she admitted.

'Not nearly so jealous as I was over your supposed husband,' Hugo assured her, his voice suddenly stark with pain as he told her, 'You don't know what that did to me, Dee, how close I came to—' He stopped. 'But I told myself there were still people who needed me, even if *you* were no longer one of them. Life has to go on. Your father knew that too, Dee.'

'Yes,' she agreed quietly. 'I believe he did.'

It was easy to let go of the past and all the pain it contained now that Hugo was here with her, holding her, loving her. She was never going to let him go again. *Never.*

Their guests had gone and Beth was stacking the dishwasher whilst Alex washed the crystal glasses which had been a gift to them from his family in Prague.

'Wasn't that the most extraordinary thing with Dee and Hugo?' Beth asked him conversationally.

'Dee and Hugo...what do you mean? What was extraordinary about them?' Alex replied, frowning. 'I admit that the fact that they already knew one another was a coincidence...'

'Oh, Alex! Surely you *must* have seen...noticed...?' Beth demanded.

'Seen *what*? They hardly spoke to one another all evening,' Alex protested.

Beth rolled her eyes.

'They didn't *need* to speak. You could practically feel the air palpitating around them.'

'Palpitating?' Alex gave an amused snort of derision. 'Hearts palpitate, Beth. Air—'

'Yes... Yes, exactly.' Beth pounced before he could finish. 'And *their* hearts were palpitating all right. There's something going on between those two,' she pronounced darkly. 'Heavens, the way they were *looking* at one another—I almost expected the air between them to self-ignite...'

Alex gave a theatrical sigh.

'Look, I don't want to dampen your hopes. I know that you, and Anna and Kelly for that matter, are so blissfully pleased with yourselves for being lucky enough to find such wonderful men, but— Ouch!' Alex protested as Beth threw a dishcloth at him.

'*We* were lucky, huh?'

'Beth, where are you going?' Alex asked her as she suddenly turned and walked towards the kitchen door.

'I'm going to ring Anna...in private...'

'You don't think that Beth guessed, do you?' Dee asked Hugo anxiously as she snuggled into his arms beneath the warmth of her duvet. 'She gave me a *very* knowing look when she said goodnight.'

'Well, if she *has* guessed it wasn't my fault,' Hugo responded virtuously. '*I* wasn't the one playing footsie under the table—and very suggestively too, I might add.'

'I've already told you that was an accident,' Dee protested. 'I'd lost my shoe...'

'Mmm, and I nearly lost *my* self-control. Anyway, what does it matter if she did guess?'

'You *know* we said that we wouldn't go public until after the committee meeting. If I'd known when she originally invited me to dinner that Alex's duty invite was you, I—'

'You mean *you* said we wouldn't go public...'

'We don't want the other members of the committee to think that—'

'That what?' Hugo teased her. 'That I'm so desperately in love with you that you used your wicked wiles to get me to vote in your favour?'

'Certainly not. I would never do anything like that,' Dee protested indignantly.

'No...? Are you sure?' Hugo wheedled coaxingly as he slid his hand over the curve of her hip.

'Mmm...I thought *I* was supposed to be the one doing the seducing,' Dee murmured huskily.

'Mmm. Well, perhaps I'm trying to use *my* wicked wiles on *you*.'

'What for?' Dee asked him softly as she opened her mouth to his kiss. 'I've already given in to you...'

'Mmm...you have, haven't you?' Hugo agreed. 'And pretty soon everyone's going to know that you have, *aren't* they?' he asked her, gently patting her stomach.

'Hugo,' Dee objected. 'How did you know?' she asked him. 'It's far too soon yet, and...'

'I know for exactly the same reason that *you* know,' Hugo told her. 'What we shared was just too powerful, too strong, too intense for us not to have created a new life together.'

'We can't be sure...' Dee warned him. 'Not yet.' But Hugo could see the hope in her eyes, and his heart melted with love for her.

'You'll have to marry me now,' he told her.

'Yes, but not until after the committee meeting,' Dee told him teasingly.

'Not until after the committee meeting,' Hugo agreed.

* * *

'And so, in conclusion, I would like to reiterate that in my view this committee has a moral obligation to the original founder of the charity to follow in his footsteps and apply charitable help to that section of the community where it is most needed. As this report in front of you proves quite conclusively, it is needed nowhere more than in the relief of the deprivation that is being suffered by the town's young people.

'To give them not just a sense of self-worth, nor even a future to look forward to, but positive and concrete proof of their town's faith and belief in them would surely be a fitting tribute to the spirit of everything that your founder stood for. By helping those young people we are *investing* in the future. Not just *their* future, but the future of our own descendants as well. To deny them the opportunity to become responsible citizens would, in my view, be a grave moral indictment of us as human beings.

'To take on a task of the magnitude of this one is a very bold and courageous step, there is no doubt about that, but I believe it is one we are capable of making. The question is, do you believe it?'

Dee gasped as Hugo sat down to a standing ovation from the whole committee.

He had completely surprised her when he had asked the committee if he might address them, not as Peter's representative but as a private individual.

Although somewhat surprised, they had agreed. Hugo's reputation had gone before him and Dee had seen how impressed they were by him.

Now, as he sat down, her eyes filled with proud tears. Here, in the shape of the words her husband-to-be, her lover, the father of her child, their child, their children, had just uttered, she had heard the vindication of everything that her father had hoped and worked for.

Hugo had put her case so well, turning it on its head so that instead of pleading with the committee to have compassion for the young of the town he had actually made them feel that they were *already* the compassionate, wise, comprehending people they must prove themselves to be.

As she looked around her she could almost sense her father's presence and his approval, his *love*. Ignoring the amazed looks of the other members of the committee, she went over to Hugo and kissed him.

'I love you,' she told him huskily. 'I love you so much.'

There was no doubt about the way the committee would vote; she could see it in their faces. Rye's young people would have their new centre and meeting place. They would learn proper trades, they would thrive and grow, and the town would thrive with them.

Tonight she was hosting a very special dinner party. Those who had been invited thought it was being given to celebrate her birthday, and that was what she wanted them to believe—Kelly and Brough, Anna and Ward, Beth and Alex.

She looked down at the diamond ring glittering on her left hand. Hugo had given it to her this morning...in bed.

Like the ring on her finger, her life had come full circle, bringing her back to the place she most wanted to be, the person she most wanted to be with. And tonight, at dinner, she would introduce Hugo to her friends as her husband-to-be, her lover. The shadows Julian Cox had thrown over her life had gone for ever. Hugo had banished them with the warmth of his love.

'Stop looking at me like that,' he warned her in a whisper against her ear as he bent his head towards her. 'Otherwise...'

The votes had been cast and the result was a resounding yes.

Dee was still looking at Hugo and whispered softly, 'Most definitely, yes.'

EPILOGUE

THE bells gave tongue, a burst of joyous, almost triumphant sound, as Dee and Hugo emerged from the church into the sunshine outside.

'Why is it that women cry at weddings?' Brough demanded as he, Ward and Alex exchanged very male looks with one another while their respective partners, to a woman, viewed the bride and groom through a happy film of tears.

'It's because we're so happy, of course,' Kelly answered him truthfully.

'So very, very happy,' Anna concurred softly as the three women looked tenderly at one another.

This morning, before the service, as the three of them had bustled about Dee's bedroom helping her to get ready, Dee had suddenly commanded them all to stop, and opened the bottle of champagne in an ice-bucket next to her dressing table, pouring four glasses.

'To love and happiness,' she had proposed, raising her glass, and then, as the other three had joined her in her toast, she had added with a wicked, very Dee-like smile, 'And to the man who is in many ways the author of the happiness we have all found in this last year or so.' Whilst the others had hesitated, her smile had deepened, and she'd enlightened them. 'Julian

Cox. Without him *none* of us would have met our wonderful, perfect partners.'

'You want to *toast* Julian Cox?' Anna had marvelled softly. 'Oh, Dee...'

'Why not?' Dee challenged her gently. 'There isn't room in my life any more for negative, destructive feelings, Anna... I don't need them...'

'Dee's right,' Kelly had confirmed. 'Julian might have cast a horribly grey and threatening cloud over all our lives in one way or another, but it quite definitely turned out to be a cloud with a silver lining.'

'Well, then, perhaps we should make our toast to hidden silver linings,' Beth had suggested.

Between them they had finished the bottle of champagne, but, watching Dee now, Anna knew that it wasn't the champagne that was responsible for the glow of happiness on her face, that open look of love with which she was regarding Hugo. The bells were still pealing, the rose petals making a silver and pink moving cloud around the bridal couple, and Dee looked radiant in her wedding gown of antique cream lace. Anna, Beth and Kelly, her three supporters-cum-attendants, were dressed in similarly elegantly styled gowns of toning cream raw silk, trimmed with the most beautiful matt dull gold cummerbunds fastened with huge soft bows at the back. The little bridesmaids, in contrast, were in the same colour combination, but their dresses were pure fairy tale—masses of cream silk voile over matt gold underskirts.

The photographers coaxed everyone together for a final photograph outside the church. That over, Dee turned to whisper something to her new husband. After giving her a tender kiss, Hugo detached himself from her and came over to where the other six were standing.

'Can you start getting everyone organised to leave for the wedding breakfast?' he asked Anna. 'Dee and I have something we want to do before we leave, so if you could cover for us for a few minutes...?'

'No problem,' Anna assured him, and she and the others started to discreetly get the guests moving.

'Do you think he knows?' Dee asked Hugo quietly as she leaned her head against his shoulder and looked down at her father's grave. She had just placed her bridal flowers on it, and as Hugo's arm tightened around her a happy tear splashed down onto the cream blooms.

'I don't know,' Hugo told her softly. 'But what I *do* know is how much, how very much, I love you, Dee...' He could feel her trembling as he kissed her. 'Come on,' he told her firmly. 'You and I have got a wedding breakfast to attend.'

'You and I?' Dee questioned, smiling at him. 'Don't you meant the three of us...?' As she turned towards him in profile it was possible to see what the elegant shaping of her gown had kept modestly concealed: the ripening shape of her body.

'The three of us,' Hugo echoed huskily, whilst outside the church the final flurry of rose petals sank gently onto the earth.

If you enjoyed what you just read,
then we've got an offer you can't resist!

Take 2 bestselling
love stories FREE!
Plus get a FREE surprise gift!

London's streets aren't just paved with gold—they're home to three of the world's most eligible bachelors!

You can meet these gorgeous men, and the women who steal their hearts, in:

NOTTING HILL GROOMS

Look out for these tantalizing romances set in London's exclusive Notting Hill, written by highly acclaimed authors who, between them, have sold more than 35 million books worldwide!

Irresistible Temptation by Sara Craven
Harlequin Presents® #2077
On sale December 1999

Reform of the Playboy by Mary Lyons
Harlequin Presents® #2083
On sale January 2000

The Millionaire Affair by Sophie Weston
Harlequin Presents® #2089
On sale February 2000

Available wherever Harlequin books are sold.

HARLEQUIN®
Makes any time special ™

Visit us at www.romance.net

HPNHG

Coming Next Month

HARLEQUIN PRESENTS®

THE BEST HAS JUST GOTTEN BETTER!

#2085 THE SEDUCTION BUSINESS Charlotte Lamb
Bianca Milne has been assigned to supervise the buyout of Matt Hearne's company. So when she offers to help look after his small daughter, she doesn't anticipate that the enforced proximity will only ignite the smoldering attraction between them....

#2086 A MAN TO MARRY Carole Mortimer
Cat wasn't interested in a brief fling! Gorgeous bachelor Caleb Reynolds was intriguing, his little son adorable. She longed to be able to surrender to his passion, but that would also mean trusting him with her well-guarded secret....

#2087 FACING UP TO FATHERHOOD Miranda Lee
(His Baby)
When a beautiful brunette wheeled a pram into Dominic Hunter's office, claiming he was the baby's father, he knew he couldn't have forgotten making love to *her!* But Tina was convinced this heartless seducer was Bonnie's dad and was determined to make him face up to fatherhood....

#2088 HUSBAND ON TRUST Jacqueline Baird
(Passion)
In the seven weeks since their whirlwind wedding, gorgeous entrepreneur Alex Solomos has transformed Lisa's life. She tells herself she's being foolish for having any doubts—until she makes two shocking discoveries....

#2089 THE MILLIONAIRE AFFAIR Sophie Weston
(Notting Hill Grooms)
Nikolai Ivanov was London's most eligible bachelor. Lisa Romaine was from the wrong side of town. But Nikolai couldn't help but be intrigued, as well as infuriated, by the provocative young woman his aunt had taken into her luxurious Notting Hill home....

#2090 MARRIAGE ON TRIAL Lee Wilkinson
On their wedding day Elizabeth had insisted on an annulment and had disappeared from Quinn Durville's life. Five years later he's tracked her down and claims she's still his wife. He wants a trial marriage. But does he really love her, or is he just out for revenge?

CNM0200